KAREN ROBERTS

THE MIRROR KNOWS WHAT THE MIRROR KNOWS.

1

For Lesley- Thank You for encouraging me to do something with my scribbles.

THE JUNK SHOP

The antique mirror was propped up against a wall, almost out of sight, gathering dust and forgotten. Occasionally the owner of the shop would notice it as he moved his stock here and there to make room for new items.

It had come into his possession as part of a job lot from a country house. Large and ornate it was certainly not something that would fit in with 21st century decor, but a call from a TV production team asking for candlesticks, mirrors and tapestries had reminded him that it was in the backroom.

He carried it to the front of the shop, dusted it and gave the glass a quick polish. Not sure how to price it he decided that he would wait and see how many other items the TV people chose and give an overall price, including the mirror.

He wondered how many young ladies had checked their appearance in this mirror before entering a ballroom or banqueting suite and how many men had straightened their ties or slicked back their hair in front of it.

Hopefully it would find a new home today.

The TV team arrived, three smartly dressed young women each holding a clip board and pen. They searched the shop, ticking off items from their list as they found them.

The shop owner followed them, mentally rubbing his hands in glee, as he removed price tags and stuck sold signs on the items they required.

Finally they stood at the door and woman in charge told the proprietor that a van would arrive later in the day to collect the goods and if he provided an itemised invoice, payment would be made by bank transfer.

'What about the mirror?' he asked. She shook her head.

'Sorry it's no good. It's slightly cloudy at the top and far too ornate for the room we are dressing at the moment.'

They left and the owner looked at the mirror, wishing they had taken it as it had been there far too long. He sighed and decided to compile the invoice before he returned it to the store room.

As he walked towards his desk the bell above the shop door rang and a young woman came in. She was wearing a long, colourful dress and had flowers woven into her braided hair. Not his normal type of customer.

He smiled and then turned his attention back to the list he was preparing, delighted to see the total mounting up.

'Excuse me,' said the woman. 'Is this mirror for sale?'

'This is my lucky day.' he thought. 'If I can get rid of it I'll not have to heave it back to the storeroom.'

'Certainly is,' he nodded, 'It's slightly cloudy at the top so I have reduced it to £20.'

'I'll take it,' she said, 'It is just what I am looking for. I can easily hide the imperfection with flowers or ribbons. It will look magnificent on my wall.'

The shop owner took her £20 note and helped load the mirror into the back of her car. She handed him a card.

'My business is called Talking Rainbows,' she said. 'I tell fortunes, do past life regressions, future life progressions and help people contact their loved ones in spirit.'

The shop owner grunted as he reluctantly pocketed the card. He would not be seeing the mirror again if it was going to somewhere weird like that!

TALKING RAINBOWS
My name is Lisa Jane and I have just signed the lease on a unit in a local indoor market and I'm calling my business 'Talking Rainbows'.

It's really little more than a cubby hole, but big enough for all I want to do there. I've painted a sign to go above my space and have two walls draped in silky material, all the colours of the rainbow. Because it is so small I decided that what I needed was a mirror, a big one that I could put on the back wall to give the illusion that my space is much larger than it really is.

The stall holder next to me recommended I visited the local junk shop to see if they had anything suitable and I was lucky enough to find a huge mirror propped up, just inside the doorway. The shop seemed anxious to get rid of it, and he helped me carry it out to my car.

I bet he has had it a long time as I can't imagine many people have space in their modern homes for such a monstrosity, and that really is a good word to describe it. I suppose I could have said, gaudy, ostentatious, tasteless, I am sure you get the picture, but as I said before it will be ideal to 'enlarge' Talking Rainbows.

My father gasped in horror when he saw it but after he had used his DIY skills to affix it to the wall and I had decorated it with colourful ribbons he agreed that it did make the space more appealing.

My promo is printed, my website is active and my Facebook page is up and running and already attracting interest.

Nearby stall holders have warned me that it could take six months to establish myself and get regular clientele. So I came up with a plan that I hope will give me some free publicity.

I contacted the local newspaper and offered a reporter a free session of past life regression in return for some positive feedback. I am very excited because they are sending someone and she will be my very first customer when I open on Saturday.

I've got my fingers crossed that the reporter's article and recommendations from future clients will bring in those wishing to take advantage of what I offer and I'll earn enough to pay the rent and give me spending money as well.

THE FIRST CLIENT

The reporter arrived at exactly 9.30 and I began to explain that I would be asking her to close her eyes and then I'd relax her by talking softly as I guided her on a journey that would take her back in time to a place she had previously lived.

The reporter nodded but before I could ask her to close her eyes I noticed some movement in front of us. It seemed as though the rainbow curtains, reflected in the mirror, had parted to reveal some figures.

A story, her story played out before our eyes.

* * * * *

THE PHOTOGRAPHS

Maria Hutchcraft, spinster of this parish, fastened the cameo pendant around her neck. She had complied with her mother's instructions as to what she should wear when the photographs were taken. So now wearing her best silk ball gown, elbow length black, lace gloves and with her hair pinned back she was ready to meet the photographer.

Her mother surveyed her as she walked sedately down the stairs.

'You look extraordinarily beautiful,' she said approvingly. '

'Herbert Preston won't be able to resist you.'

Maria sighed. This latest scheme of her mother's, to secure a suitor for her, would hopefully never come to fruition.

Her elder brother, John, and his wife had both tried to persuade Mrs Hutchcraft that a widower of forty-seven was not an ideal match for the fun loving, twenty year old Maria. Their arguments had barely been listened to. Mrs Hutchcraft wanted Maria off her hands as soon as possible.

'That girl's had too much freedom. The sooner she is married and has the responsibility of a husband and a house to care for the better,' she'd told them as she left the room.

'It's all down to her vanity,' John explained to his sister.

'She doesn't want to be seen as the only mother round here with an unmarried daughter. Have the photographs taken and keep your fingers crossed that by the time they reach Mother's cousin Herbert in Australia he will have found himself a bride.'

When Maria and her mother entered the garden the photographer was standing on the lawn, waiting patiently with his camera already fixed onto a tripod.

'I suggest you stand in front of those magnificent trees,' he said, pointing to two apple trees that were covered in pink blossom.

'They will make an excellent backdrop for the photographs.'

Maria shrugged. She thought the whole exercise was a waste of time and money. Money they really hadn't got to spare on such a crazy idea.

Ever since the death of her father three months earlier and the news that he had gambled away most of the family's wealth Mrs Hutchcraft had been scheming to find a husband for Maria.

But honestly would Herbert Preston, thousands of miles away in Australia, take her as his wife simply from seeing her photograph? Just his old fashioned name sent shivers up and down her spine.

Mrs Hutchcraft was annoying the photographer. She kept issuing instructions to her daughter.

'Maria stand up straight.'

'Maria you need to smile.'

'Maria look at the camera not the tree.'

'Please Mrs. Hutchcraft,' said the photographer, 'informal photographs are far more flattering and reveal more of a subject's character than formal studio portraits. Maybe as it is such a hot afternoon it would be better if you retired indoors out of the sun and then we can continue.'

Mrs Hutchcraft refused to leave the garden and continued to shout directions to her daughter.

'With all due respect Madam,' said the photographer, 'I cannot do my job with you interfering like this. If you wish me to continue I must ask you to return indoors.'

Mrs Hutchcraft was not pleased but there was no time to dismiss the impertinent man and find another photographer. She needed the photos to be sent to her cousin as soon as possible, before he found himself an Australian wife.

Having issued a final demand that when he'd finished outside he took some formal pictures of Maria in the ballroom she relented and went into the house.

Maria relaxed as the photographer engaged her in conversation. First politely remarking on the weather then enquiring if the photos were for her debutant season.

Maria shook her head explaining about her mother's widower cousin in Australia and the plan to send her there as his bride.

The photographer was truly shocked at the idea of this beautiful young woman being sent to an unknown middle aged husband and lifestyle on the other side of the world.

They chatted and laughed as he took the photos.

They met secretly while the photos were being processed.

They planned their future.

Three weeks later, while Mrs Hutchcraft was admiring the photos of her daughter, carefully mounted in a leather bound album, and while she was choosing which ones to sent to her cousin, Maria and the photographer slipped away to Gretna Green.

* * * * *

THE REPORTER

As the image died away I looked at my client. She was staring at the mirror.

'I saw it all happen,' she said.' 'Did you see it?'

I nodded

'I saw it as though it was being projected and the mirror was the screen, and I heard what was being said,' she said. 'I recognised the garden and those two apple trees.'

'Maybe you lived there in a previous life,' I suggested.

She shook her head.

'No, I was that photographer, I remember it all so clearly, how cross I was with that interfering old lady, how beautiful the young woman was and,' she stopped talking and drew in a deep breath. 'Look at me now," she said, pointing at her expensive digital SLR camera, 'I am still taking photos.'

'I went back to that garden,' she continued, 'I know I did. I went back with Maria who was my wife and we had two small children with us. My mother in law never liked me for stealing her daughter's heart, and ruining her plans for Maria to be married to some relative.'

I tried to explain to the reporter that this was not the usual way my past life session were conducted but I don't think she was really listening. She took some photos of me and of the room and asked me to let her know if a similar experience happened to any more of my clients. Then she left.

Even though I contacted her to say that two more people had seen previous lives in the mirror there was no article about Talking Rainbows, in the next edition of the paper and I was disappointed.

However, two weeks later I was delighted to see the paper had printed a full page spread entitled, "I know who I was in 1876."

The reporter explained in her article exactly what had happened with the mirror during her session and then revealed that since her visit she had been busy doing some genealogical research and now had the marriage certificate for Maria Hutchcraft, spinster, and Peter Durford, a photographer. The witnesses were Ethel Hutchcraft (bride's mother) and John Hutchraft (bride's brother). She had also discovered they had two children, a girl called Sylvia and a boy named Matthew.

The article concluded by saying this was an amazing experience and recommended a visit to Talking Rainbows for anyone who wished to know about a past life.

As you can imagine I have been very busy ever since that article was published and offer you, in story form, some of the experiences I shared with my clients during the month of June. N.B. In the stories that follow all names and locations have been changed to preserve anonymity of my clients, who have all given permission for their session to be transcribed and made public.

THE SCEPTIC

A young man, dressed in blue denim jeans and a blue shirt, came by one day last week and asked to book for the following Tuesday.

'I am interested to know what you will tell me, he said, 'because I am 100% sure I have never been here before, but my fiancé insists we have all had previous lives. She says because she was a fireman in her last life and lumber jack before that she has reincarnated as a woman this time to experience feminine energy. '

'Sometimes I think her ideas are totally crazy,' he added with a smile.

I settled him in the chair, facing the mirror and explained the traditional way of doing a regression, but as before a story was projected onto the mirror, this time in the form of a blue orb which started to speak.

* * * * *

THE BLUE ORB
'I am a blue orb just pulsating in time with all the similar structures around me. None of us move. We do not eat or drink. We communicate our thoughts by

what you would call singing. We vocalise them melodically.

We are capable of sensing what is happening around the Universe.

I don't have a name or a number. I am just me. I am tuned into Planet Earth and my job is to report back all I see to The Hierarchy of The Cosmos. I wasn't present when your world began and I will not be here when this planet dies.

You may think this is not much of a life but I can assure you that you were happy when you were me.'

* * * * *

The image faded and I saw my client had tears in his eyes.

'Thank you,' he said. 'It seems I *have* had a previous life but it was not here on Planet Earth.'

'That explains so much, you see I have what I suppose you could call a fixation with the colour blue. All my clothes are blue, my bedroom is painted blue and all the bedding is that colour too. My car is blue and I have just had a row with my fiancé because she has chosen a white wedding dress but I really wanted her to have a blue one. I suppose I knew deep down she wouldn't agree so I tried to get her to compromise and have the bridesmaids dressed in blue, but sadly she insists their dresses will be pink and my tie has to match them.'

He wiped his eyes, paid me and said, 'I guess I owe Marina an apology. I am going to tell her about this straightaway so she will understand why I am addicted to the colour blue and maybe she'll change her mind about those dresses.'

He hurried out of Talking Rainbows with a smile on his face.

THE WATER PHOBIC LADY
Carole Jones contacted me because she had heard that sometimes an insight into a past life can help resolve a problem in the life you are living now.

I told her I could not guarantee that would happen but we could certainly try. The result was very interesting.

The curtains reflected in the mirror kept swishing open and closed as different scenes played out in front of us.

* * * * * *

<u>1998</u>. Jean Connell threw her hands in the air in despair.

'Same old story,' she sighed.

'Still refusing to get in the bath?' the health visitor enquired.

'Absolutely.' replied Jean, 'Water would never touch this child if I didn't struggle to wash her every day. I remember the nurse in the delivery room saying she'd never seen a baby being born with a smile on its face. I've wondered since if she was just so please to be out of all that water in the womb.'

Both women laughed.

<u>1206</u> The Lord was due at daybreak. The decree proclaiming, 'All females aged between fourteen and twenty-one must assemble in front of the church at dawn tomorrow,' had been read out in the church on Sunday.

It was a decree that brought fear into everyone's hearts. Never before had the

Lord sent a lackey with such disturbing instructions. Loath to leave their girls alone, whole families stood and waited in silent huddles.

They saw a dust cloud on the horizon and knew he was coming. Their Lord and Master, who so rarely passed through the village, was on his way and everyone knew this visit would bring grief to at least one family.

He rode into the churchyard with two attendants who dismounted and then held his horse as he slowly swung himself to the ground. He was old and arthritic. He spoke to his servants who moved quickly through the crowd separating the frightened girls from their families.

The Lord shuffled over, surveying each girl as he passed. Suddenly, he stopped in front of Kitty Holmes and placed a hand on her shoulder.

'You shall be my bride,' he said.

Kitty's eyes widened with fear. She curtseyed.

Sire,' she whispered, 'I am betrothed.'

'To me," said the Lord, reaching out for her hand. Kitty shrank away from his touch.

No Sire, to Ben Roberts,' she said.

The Lord snapped his fingers and a servant quickly lifted the terrified girl onto his horse and mounted behind her.

Kitty struggled and screamed as the horse started to move. In slow motion she watched as her fiancé tried to stop the horse from leaving the churchyard, only to be pushed aside by the Lord's other servant. She heard Ben cursing and her mother and sister crying.

She was aware of the silence of the other villagers. They were shocked yet relieved their daughters were safe.

As the horse picked up speed, Kitty tried to free herself from the servant's grasp.

'Let me go,' she begged, 'Please let me go.'

The Lord came galloping up and as he drew abreast of them he shouted to the hysterical girl, 'Silence. Cease that noise at once or your family will suffer.'

Kitty was too distraught to understand his words and continued to try and free herself.

The Lord bellowed them again and this time she heard and understood. She fell forward, limp and frightened for her future.

When they reached the castle the Lord ordered food for the girl and demanded she be brought to his quarters when she had been fed.

Close up he was even more terrifying to the poor girl. His head was bald, his face lined with wrinkles and the hand that beckoned her forward was gnarled and bony.

<u>2001</u>.' I'm going to the seaside tomorrow,' Carole informed her Grandmother, 'and there will be sand, sea and buckets and spades.'

'I am sure you'll have a lovely time,' said her Gran. Secretly wondering how hydrophobic Carole would fare on discovering the sea was composed of water.

The postcard that arrived later in the week explained it all.

'Weather magnificent. Carole took one look at the sea, announced it was made of water, and refused to even go on the beach.'

<u>1206</u> Kitty was unable to move. The Lord gestured to the servant who dragged her roughly across the floor and pushed her into the chair beside his master. Kitty trembled as a bony finger pointed directly at her head.

'You are a lucky girl,' the Lord said.

'You must forget your fiancé and your family as I have chosen you to be my new wife. I expect, in fact I demand you give me a son and in return I will feed and clothe you and make sure your family live in peace and safety and never go hungry. Disobey me and produce nothing but wenches and your family will suffer and you will be cast out like that last wife of mine. Do you understand?'

Too frightened to reply Kitty sat in silence. The lord jabbed his skeletal finger against her forehead.

'DO YOU UNDERSTAND,' he bellowed. Kitty nodded in silence as her plans for a happy life with Ben faded slowly away, replaced by the reality she now knew was her future.

2016 Carole was getting hotter and hotter as she lay on the recliner under the midday sun. She heaved a sigh of regret, wishing she could join her friends who were splashing, swimming and floating in the warm water, but just the sight of the pool made her feel uneasy. She wished she knew why she felt like this.

1210 Kitty, heavily pregnant with her third child, wandered up to the battlements. She offered up a prayer that this time she would give birth to a son.

She watched the gulls circling around the small harbour. She dreamt of the day, hopefully in seven months, when she would hear the words, 'It's a boy,' signifying that her ordeal was over and she would be free from the advances of her elderly controlling husband.

She glanced down at the water swirling around the castle walls. As usual she felt the pull of the deep, the urge to fling herself from this height down, down, down into the dark water below.

To the dismay of the lord their first child was a girl and so was the second. He banished both children to the hovel where Kitty's parents lived.

Periodically he sent his servants with food for the impoverished family but there had never enough to feed them and the two baby girls.

The lord was forever telling Kitty he was tired of siring useless females but he had promised her one more chance to provide him with an heir.

However if this third offspring was not a boy, Kitty her three girls and her whole family would be banished from their home and from the village. She knew this would be a disaster for them all.

The water called to her. She watched the waves- she felt fear, they were physically tugging at her heart. They were calling to her, waiting for her, trying to rescue her, offering a chance to escape.

She felt torn in two, wanting desperately to answer their call. What was the lesser of two evils? Should she choose the dark, deep water before her or life with the evil lord?

2018 Carole saw the article while browsing the local paper.

'I know who I was in 1876'

She glanced at it and turned the page to see what films the local cinema was showing. Then she turned back to the article. Under it here was an advert for Talking Rainbows the place where the reporter had been and in the small print she read. 'Being regressed to a time in a previous life where a phobia originated can often resolve the problem you may be having in this present life.'

<u>1211</u> She feared the water. Its power over her was growing stronger each time she walked along the battlements. She was mesmerised by the waves, their sound, their dark water and the possibility that they offered her of peace from heartache, fear and cruelty.

In the early hours of July 6th 1211 Kitty went into labour

'Your good health sire,' those assembled at the lord's table said in unison as they raised their goblets.

Sir Percy signalled to the serving wench and more flagons of wine were brought to refill the drinking vessels.

An old woman slipped into the room where the men were drinking. She whispered into Sir Percy's ear. He smiled, fumbled in his clothing and extracted a coin which he handed to her.

Slowly he rose to his feet, lifted his goblet and said, 'Please rise and drink to the good health of my son John Edward Percy.'

Later some of the revellers staggered as they stood, some remained seated, unable to get to their feet, as toast followed toast throughout the evening.

The housekeeper obeyed instructions, employed a wet nurse for the child, packed up all Kitty's meagre possessions and arranged for a cart to deliver her back to her family. Her job was done and the lord did not wish to see her again.

Kitty was delighted to be free and to see her family again, especially her beloved daughters.

She was dismayed to discover Ben Roberts was happily married and with three daughters of his own and that the stress of the preceding years had taken its toll on her weary parents.

She helped about the house, delighting in the chatter of her children and her freedom.

But many times she strayed down to the shore, looking hopefully up at the castle for a glimpse of her son and staring fearfully at the water which was still trying to entice her into its dark depths.

* * * * *

Suddenly the mirror reflected nothing but the rainbow curtains, all the images had gone. I looked at my client. Her face was white and she was clutching the sides of the chair.

'I saw what happened to me in the 13th century.' she said.

'I was trapped in a life of brutality and abuse. The water was calling out to me, offering me a way to end my suffering. It frightened me because I really wanted to go into that water but something stopped me.'

'That maybe where your phobia of water began,' I said, 'and it has been trapped in your DNA ever since. Don't rush away from here and jump into the nearest river, just take it slowly and see if this experience has helped you in any way. Think about what you have seen and maybe get some counselling to help you understand the problem'

Carole took my advice and sought help and in August she sent me some pictures of her swimming in the sea with dolphins, a video of her squealing with delight as she jumped into a pool and another of her smiling on board a yacht, surrounded by miles and miles of water.

 I like to have fresh flowers on my table every week and I buy them from a nearby stall in the market. The owner, Jane McAdam, asked if she could book a session with me, having heard so much about my mirror and the stories it was telling.
The image was slow to appear in front of us and I wondered if I would have to do a standard regression for Jane, but gradually a story began to unfold.
* * * * *

THE BEE KEEPER
Everyone in the village was intrigued by the lady who had moved into the cottage next to the church.

   Straightaway she began the task of taming the wilderness that had grown up in the garden during the three years the house had been empty.

   The nettles were shoulder high, the ivy was entwined round trees, shrubs and garden ornaments. The once geometric box hedge needed a drastic prune.

She was a very private person, spending her weekdays tending the garden and her Sundays hidden from view of those attending church.

As she systematically cleared the weeds and undergrowth, she dug the soil and planted flowers and vegetables. Her colourful garden became a paradise for wildlife. There were squirrels and birds in the trees, hedgehogs snuffling in the borders and frogs and toads in her pond. She allowed dandelions, buttercups and daisies to grow among the grass on her lawn so there was always butterflies and moths fluttering around the flowers.

The people walking through the churchyard peered over the wall and marvelled at the size of her cabbages and lettuce.

No one knew her name so the villagers called her 'The Green Fingered Lady'.

She could often be seen just standing amid her flowers. Some said they had heard her talking and singing to her plants, others said she was a witch. Occasionally she would catch the eye of a passerby and raise her hand in greeting, but she never spoke.

One day all the curtains in nearby houses were twitching as the nosey neighbours watched a horse and cart stop outside the green fingered lady's house. They were surprised to see three wicker beehives being unloaded and then carefully carried into the garden.

Later in the year a table appeared outside the cottage gate and on it were twelve jars of honey arranged in a circle on a check table cloth.

Next to the jars The Lady With Green Fingers placed a notice saying, 'Honey for sale 3d a jar. I am a friend of the bees, are you?'

By teatime all the jars had been sold, but still no one knew the lady's name.

* * * * *

'That was me, I know it was,' said Jane.

'I have always loved bees. My brother was terrified of them because he was once stung by a wasp when he was eating an apple and after that he was frightened of any insect that buzzed around him. I always told him bees are our friends and as you know I just love flowers, and I wish my garden was big enough for me to have some hives'

'I wonder when I was that lady?'

'I'm no expert,' I replied, 'but it was in a time when they used horses and carts to move things and from the way you were dressed I think it may have been in the late 1800s. One thing we know for sure, it was many years before decimalization,' and we both laughed.

Jane was impressed and told many of her customers about her experience. Several came and booked sessions with me. One of them was Colin Drury who visited Jane's stall every Friday to buy flowers for his wife. He booked a session as a surprise for her and asked if could come with her.

* * * * *

THE KNIGHT

Sir Horrocks surveyed his armour as it lay in a large wooden chest in the hallway. Young Piers, his squire had done a good job polishing it and he hoped the joints were well oiled as it wouldn't bode well with the ladies if he creaked every time he moved.

He sauntered over to the stables where Piers was grooming his chestnut mare Willow even though he wasn't riding her today.

No today he would be astride Thunder who was already clad in his master's colours and was waiting for him to arrive.

Thunder was a pure bred stallion who could toss his head and make his mane flow better than the hair of any maiden in a temper. Sir Horocks loved this beast with his haughty manner, the heights he could jump and the speed with which he could travel

But today was all about appearance. When he entered the castle courtyard, dressed in his armour, he wanted to look magnificent, so magnificent that Lord Portland would offer him the hand of his daughter in marriage.

THE LADY- She had fallen in love with his image the very first time she saw him, his armour polished and shining in the sunlight and his plumed helmet concealing what she imagined was a handsome face.

She enjoyed watching the giant strides he took when walking and the skill he showed when riding his huge stallion.

She hoped he would glance her way. This mystery knight, who arrived every year to compete in the annual jousting tournaments held in the castle grounds, and who made the hearts of all the ladies flutter when he rode towards his opponent at high speed.

They called him Sir Gallant, though no one knew his true identity. Each year after he was crowned the victor in all the challenges he rode away from the castle and did not appear again for twelve months.

The crowd fell silent as he rode into the courtyard.

She hoped he'd win as he had in previous years. She always gave him a favour when he broke his lance on a rival's shield, a ribbon or a scarf, and another favour when he unseated a fellow competitor.

During the winter months she had stitched a handkerchief especially for him.

She dreamt of him asking her father for her hand in marriage.

This year her dream came true.

* * * * *

As the mirror misted over Colin turned to his wife.

'Remember, the first time we met I told you that I felt I knew you from somewhere and now I know why.'

He kissed her hand. 'That was me in the armour and you were the lady I married.'

THE ESKIMO

A young woman arrived for her session. 'Let's get on with it,' she said, 'I've heard so much about you and this mirror I want to see it for myself.'

We sat down and she stared at the mirror. I began to talk to her but the reflection of my rainbow walls did not change.

The woman started to get impatient. 'Have I come all this way for nothing?' she asked. 'Start your mirror working.'

'I don't know how the mirror works,' I told her. 'I don't control it.'

'Maybe it is not able to show past lives to everyone who comes. However, your journey isn't wasted as I can relax you and take you back to a previous life in the conventional way.'

'But I've come to see your supposedly magic mirror,' she grumbled, 'I could have gone to see a local hypnotherapist if that's all you are going to do.'

'I offer a past life regression session to people who come,' I said'

'I make no promises that the session will involve a mirror and I am perfectly happy to give you a conventional session.'

Rather grudgingly she said, 'Go on then get started.'

I did my normal procedure and took her over a bridge that led her back in time.

* * * * *

'Look around you what can you see?' I asked.

'Snow and ice, I am sitting on ice. I have a fishing line in my hand and I am fishing through a hole in the ice.'

'What are you wearing?' I asked.

'Everything I'm wearing is made of fur. 'My trousers, my jacket, my hat, even my boots are fur, but I am very cold, so very cold.'

'Do you know why you are sitting there? ' I said.

'We have nothing to eat. I can't go back to the igloo. I must stay here until I catch something or my wife and children will starve, but my body aches because I am so very cold.'

* * * * *

She was shivering and starting to get very upset so I brought her back over the bridge to the present time, hoping she would not be dissatisfied with the regression.

She opened her eyes and sat in silence, shaking her head from side to side.

41

Finally she spoke. 'I suffer from cold urticaria,' she said,' and when I am in a low temperature I get red welts on my skin and I itch. I have to carry an epi pen to inject myself when it happens. The doctors I've seen have no idea what causes it in some people and not in others but I think I have just discovered why I suffer from it.'

Of course I have no idea if there is any connection between her past life as an Eskimo and her present medical condition but she went away much happier than when she arrived.

My next client was a young man who had a guitar case slung across his body. He slipped it off and sat in the chair.

* * * * *

THE COCONUT GATHERER

Instantly the mirror started to shine and we were transported to what looked to me like a Caribbean beach. The sand was almost white, the sea was blue and there were coconut trees along the shore line.

Several islanders were grouped around these trees. Some had used ropes to climb high up the smooth trunks and were sitting among the branches, tapping the clusters of nuts and listening for a hollow sound that indicated they were ripe and ready for harvesting.

The men were using their knives to cut off the nuts and then they threw them down to the people waiting on the beach below.

Suddenly one of the young men slipped and fell out the tree.

* * * * *

Instantly my client started to gasp as though in pain and his forehead was covered in sweat.

I asked him if he was alright but before he could answer the scene in the mirror vanished and for a second or two it was completely blank .

Then it cleared again.

* * * * *

The young man was limping along the sand.

We watched him as he approached the coconut trees. He stood looking up into the high branches and shook his head. He turned to the men who were watching him.

'I dare not climb again. My left leg is still weak and my left arm is almost useless and if I'm honest I am too frightened to even try.'

The scene faded again and the guitarist sat in stunned silence.

* * * * *

Just for an instant I felt his pain,' he said.

'I am terrified of heights, so frightened, I won't even go in a plane,' and he added, 'people are always confused when they see me playing the guitar, They say I'm playing it backwards, and I suppose it looks as though I am. You see I was born with a slightly deformed left arm and it is easier for me to hold the instrument with my right arm and play the notes with my left.'

Quite an exhausting morning!

I realised I had just got time for a slice of pizza from the nearby stall, before the first of my afternoon clients was due to arrived.

I was looking forward to see what would happen, as Fiona had specifically requested a future life progression, hoping to gain insight into how a problem she was having with her work could possibly be resolved.

I told her, as I tell all my clients who want a future life progression, that what they learn will be just one of a possible future in store for them.

I could hear the sound of the sea before she had even sat down and as we looked towards the mirror the noise became louder and we watched as a car appeared with Fiona in the driver's seat.

* * * * *

THE FUTURE FOR FIONA.

Fiona's heart sank as she pulled her car into the parking bay.

The advert hadn't lied. The caravan *was* close to the beach and it was surrounded by grass, but how, she wondered, had the promo photo been taken to avoid showing all the other caravans sharing her view of the sea, and also, apparently, her grassy patch?

She opened the car door and took a deep breath. Yes she could smell the sea, but also the bacon frying in the caravan on her right.

She'd expected to hear the sound of waves breaking on the shore but that was impossible due to the heavy thud of a bass guitar emanating through the open windows from the caravan to her left.

'This is could be the beginning of fourteen days in Hell,' she thought, 'however will I be able to work here?'

She was contemplating getting back in the car and seeking the tranquillity she needed elsewhere when suddenly the music stopped and the door of the adjoining caravan burst open.

She blinked in surprise as a tall stranger, his dread locks shaking wildly, began waving at her.

'Hi,' he called, and leaping from his van he advanced with his right hand outstretched.

'Kevin McCloy', he announced.

'Be churlish not to respond,' thought Fiona.

'I am Fiona Strange,' she said as she shook his hand.

'So glad to have a neighbour,' said Kevin, 'Can I make you a drink?'

Fiona was tempted to say, 'No leave me alone. I didn't come here to socialise.

I've got a novel to finish, very little time to do it in and no idea how to end it.'

Instead she replied, 'That's kind of you, but I need to unpack and start work. I came here for some peace and quiet so would it be possible for you to switch off your music or at least turn it down?'

Kevin shrugged and went back to his van. The music continued, though thankfully, not as loud as before.

Over the next three days Fiona settled into a routine. She soon realised her selfish neighbour had no intention of living without his music. So each morning, as soon as the annoying beat started up, she headed down to the beach with a picnic in her backpack and a note book in her hand.

She spent her days walking along the sand, sitting on a rock staring out to the horizon and lazing among the sand dunes.

The sound of the sea was soothing, the weather was gorgeous but inspiration and the urge to write were just not there. In the late afternoons she returned to her caravan and tried to relax by reading a book, feeling envious of the lucky author who had been able to complete their novel.

She saw nothing of her neighbour, just heard his infernal music.

By 9 o'clock on Wednesday morning Fiona could still hear the waves pounding up the beach. Strange! There was no music.

'Great, I'll take a quick walk then come back and start work,' Fiona thought, but as she walked towards the beach she heard the sound of Kevin's music.

The nearer she got the louder it became and then she saw the reason why. Kevin was sitting on her favourite rock swaying to the beat of his music.

Fiona felt furious. As if she didn't have enough problems without that man and his incessant music intruding her every waking moment.

She strolled in the opposite direction contemplating the impasse she had reached with her novel. Jess, the heroine was down on her luck, had dropped out of art college, after ending her fiery relationship with Martin Pears, and had no financial means of support until the world discovered her artistic talent and people were queuing up to buy her paintings.

Reaching the far end of the bay Fiona turned to walk back. She could see

Kevin still gyrating to his music. When he spotted her, he stood up, and began walking towards her.

'Fancy seeing you here,' he said. 'It's alright for some, strolling along the beach while some of us poor creatures try to earn a living.'

Fiona frowned, 'You call jiggling around on a rock listening to that noise a job? I'll have you know I came to the caravan for some peace and quiet and hopefully some inspiration. But thanks to your ear- piercing music I've been forced to try to work on the beach and now today I find you and your noise sitting on my favourite rock.'

Kevin looked affronted.

'Believe me I'm also trying to work. REALLY TRYING, 'he shouted.

He looked sheepish and turned off his IPod.

'''I'll let you into a secret. I'm suffering from artist's block. I was hoping music and the sea breezes would clear my head but so far my mind is as blank as when I arrived last week and I'm supposed to be illustrating a children's book about a mermaid.'

Fiona smiled, 'Snap!' she said, 'I've a penniless 22 year old girl facing social disgrace and I've only three weeks to rescue her. I truly don't know how to make that happen, and I've been paid a huge advance, which I've spent and which the publishers will probably demand back if I don't meet my deadline.'

'We need coffee and some of my cake,' said Kevin.

Several hours later, after many cups of coffee had been drunk and slices of cake eaten, Fiona returned to her caravan, clutching her notebook containing a list of scribbled ideas:

Jess flees to seaside in deep depression.

She sits on a rock, doodling on her sketch pad.

Handsome man with dreadlocks strolls past.

He recognises her talent and changes her life.

Fiona left Kevin surrounded by sheets of paper, all covered in sketches of her in various poses. In each one she had a mermaid's tail!

* * * * *

The picture in the mirror vanished. Six months after Fiona had that reading I received a promotional leaflet from Wilson's Book stores advertising a nationwide book signing by Fiona

Strange, author of "Beachcombing," and it coincided with a reading in the children's department of the picture book, "The Mermaid's Pearl Necklace," illustrated by Kevin McCoy.

The author and artist had apparently insisted they wanted to travel together!

My first client on Tuesday was also interested in having a future life progression. She had recently applied to do a teacher training course but was unsure if this was the right thing for her to be considering.

'Let's see if the mirror reveals a future for you as a teacher,' I said as we sat down, facing the end wall of my cabin. This is what we saw and heard.

* * * * * *

THE OUTING

The children were very excited when I told them about our forthcoming excursion. One of them shouted out, 'That'll be better than sitting in front of a screen seeing facts about chemicals and calculating boring mathematical problems.'

This was to be their first outing. They had never been outside the complex in their whole lives. I ushered them into a lift, some were quite fearful. Of course they had seen the outside, a barren, lifeless desert, moving sand dunes and vivid blue skies, through the transparent windows

The Experience Museum had only recently been completed and we were booked in today for a lesson on rain. None of the children had seen water fall from the sky and if I am honest my memories of actually seeing rain are rather hazy.

Of course I had heard my parents and some of the older members of our community talking about days when so much of this rain fell from the sky you had to wear special clothing to keep dry.

In a large room the children were each given a strange looking object. It had a long handle with a colourful canopy attached to it. The guardian of the museum told them it was an umbrella and they laughed as they practiced saying the strange word.

'Look up at the ceiling,' he said and instead of the normal clear blue sky that we were used to, there were strange shapes moving around above us and as we watched they changed from white, to grey and then black.
'These are clouds and they are made up of lots of drops of water,' he explained.

52

I could see some of the children were looking confused, after all as far as they were aware, water was made in factories not in the sky.

'Hold the umbrella over your head,' he instructed them. The children were puzzled but did as they were told. Then to their surprise water started to drip down from the ceiling. It landed on the umbrella with a pitter patter sound and ran off onto the floor, where it instantly evaporated.

'That was just a light shower,' explained the guardian, "It was called drizzle.'

Again some of the children laughed at the unusual word.

'Now keep your umbrellas over your head and you will now feel what it was like during a heavy rain storm.'

Some of the children shrieked with fear as the water droplets pounded onto their umbrellas, but it was over in just two or three minutes, and everywhere was suddenly lit up by a bright light.

'Come out from under your umbrellas,' said the guardian and look up at the sky.'

The children did as they were told and arcing over us was a magnificent rainbow. They gasped in wonder and I suddenly remembered a time long ago before The Trouble when my parents and I were having a picnic. There had been a short unexpected shower of rain and then as the sun burst through the clouds my mother had pointed out the colours in the sky.

'You are very lucky,' she said, 'because you have just seen a rainbow.'

I also recalled that day was when my parents, Rachel and Barry, told me how they had met.

Apparently my father had lent her one of these strange umbrellas when he saw her about to leave the office building during a heavy rain shower and wearing a summer dress and no coat.

'Here take my umbrella,' he'd said, 'I've got a jacket and am picking up a taxi outside so I won't need it.'

He, Barry, was one of the bosses, admired for his good looks by Rachel and all her friends in the typing pool. She took the umbrella and felt excited when she realised she would have to give it back sometime, and that would give her an excuse to talk to him.

It was two whole weeks before it rained again and Rachel could put her 'return the umbrella plan' into operation. She put on her raincoat, picked up her bag and lifted the large black umbrella from the hook where it had been stored for the past fortnight.

Opening the front door she watched the rain sheeting down in front of her. If she used his umbrella it would be very wet when she handed it back but if she didn't she would arrive like the proverbial drowned rat and he would wonder why she hadn't thought to shelter under it.

She had really not thought this through. Maybe it would have been a better idea to return it straight away on a fine day. Too late for that now, this was decision time!

She pulled the hood up on her raincoat, unfurled the black umbrella, and headed off towards the bus stop. As the bus approached she lowered the umbrella, shook off the raindrops and smiled as she boarded the bus.

In ten minutes, if all went to plan she would be knocking on his office door and when he told her to enter she intended to ask him if she could buy him a drink for his kindness in lending her his umbrella.

That evening they had the first of many dates.

* * * * *

The client was happy that her decision
to train as a teacher was the right one,
though slightly confused as to whether
what she had just seen would take place
during this lifetime, after an apparent
trouble had occurred on earth,
disrupting the climate, or in a new life
many years from now.

I didn't hear from her again so I am
not sure if she actually trained as a
teacher.

THE REENACTOR
A young man phoned to ask if a future
life progression session can show you
something in your immediate future. He
was organising a banquet for an English
Civil War re-enactment group.

'It is something we have never tried
before,' he explained, 'and I thought it
would be exciting to incorporate a
murder mystery into our annual
regimental banquet and to hold it at
Halloween.

I have booked a castle as the venue
and my brother in law, Donald, who is a
historian, has helped me write a script.
Everyone booked to attend has been
assigned a character and will be given
details of their daily life. I don't know
why but I'm having second thoughts

about going ahead with the whole thing. A work colleague said you may be able to help.'

He booked an appointment and it was a VERY interesting session!

* * * * *

THE INTRUDERS AT THE BANQUET

Clampet Castle, renowned for the Roundhead siege that claimed many lives during the English Civil War was chosen as the sinister venue for the banquet and the 'murders"

Arriving late Joan Wyatt and her family realised the party had already started.

Joan looked around the large hall. 'Who are those people?' she whispered loudly to her daughter, pointing to a nearby group of revellers.

'They must be new recruits, 'Alice replied looking puzzled, 'I don't recognise any of them.'

Joan limped over to greet the strangers.

'Joan Wyatt,' she boomed, 'in charge of regimental living history. This is Alice, my daughter, and Maddie, my granddaughter. My son, Chris, is here somewhere. He came earlier to organise things. He's the membership secretary. And you are?'

The strangers glared at Joan, said nothing, and turned away.

Desperate for information Joan looked around for Chris. He hadn't said there were new recruits. That was very remiss of him. He knew she like to be informed when new families joined The Regiment.

As Joan searched for her son four musketeers approached carrying a man's body by its arms and legs.

'Drunk already,' scoffed Joan, 'and the banquet has barely begun. I can't imagine what you'll be like by the end of the evening'

Unbeknown to the latecomers there'd already been a 'murder', and the body being manhandled towards them was that of the elusive Chris.

'Make way! Make way!' called out Terry Wilkes, one of the musketeers.

Alice suddenly realised what was happening and stifled a giggle in case her dominating mother saw her smiling.

With a wicked look in his eye Terry called out again, 'Oh Mistress Wyatt. It's with great sorrow I must tell you that we are carrying the body of your only son. 'He was struck down when a dagger was plunged straight into his heart.'

As he was carried by Chris winked at his sister and daughter.

Joan's confusion turned to anger.

'This is ridiculous! Chris is the organiser. How can he make sure everyone has a good time if he's a murder victim?'

'It makes sense to me,' said Maddie, defending her father.

' I'm guessing 'dying' so early gives him time to organise the other murders,'

'Let's find our rooms,' said Alice, 'put on our authentic clothes and join in the fun with the rest of the regiment.'

Taking hold of her mother's arm Alice guided her over the uneven cobbles to their quarters, helped her put on the elaborate banqueting gown and pinned on a badge which stated, ' Mistress Mary. Owner of the local tavern'.

Then Alice slipped into her own 17th century costume and attached her name badge. 'Alice, serving wench at The Black Bull.'

Maddie's label said, 'Maddie, a lowly housemaid at the castle'

Alice helped her mother hobble back to the festivities where people were drinking and singing, in true re-enactment tradition.

Still fretting about the strangers Joan was annoyed that no one else seemed bothered by their presence.

Chris, now dressed as a monk, came over to his mother.

He bent down and whispered in her ear, 'I'm in disguise so I can mingle and organise the next murders. I'm sure Alice will want to dance after we've eaten so I'll come and escort you to the ballroom so you can watch.'

'Just who are those strangers? When did they join and why are they here?' demanded Joan, 'They ignored me when I tried to talk to them. They're very rude! '

Chris shook his head in exasperation at his Mother's words.

'I have no idea but I'm guessing they joined at the last muster. The one we missed because of Maddie's graduation. Strange though, because I thought the banquet was fully booked before that event.'

He shook his head again.

'Anyway I must go as Jeff Bines is due to 'die' very soon and I need to organise the props for his demise.'

Joan turned to Alice.

'How inconsiderate of Donald to be away again when we have an event,' she grumbled. 'You should tell him to rearrange his work so he can come with us. A husband should be with his wife at an event like this.'

'Although your father enjoyed the battles he wasn't fond of the winter banquets, but I expected him to come with me and he always did.'

Alice sighed, unable to tell her mother that Donald, her even tempered husband, who seemed to love everyone no matter what they said or did, simply could not abide Joan and her constant meddling in their lives. He always made sure that work commitments took him away from home whenever a Civil War reenactment was scheduled that Joan was due to attend. The thought of a whole weekend in such close proximity to his mother in law filled him with horror.

Alice didn't mention that the other monk, helping Chris orchestrate the murders, was actually Donald, disguised so he could join in the fun while keeping his distance from the cantankerous Joan.

At a signal from Chris, events were set in motion for the next 'murder'.

As the supposedly unsuspecting Jeff opened a booby trapped door, a sack fell on him and he crumpled to the ground. Hidden behind the door, Donald pressed 'play' on his phone releasing a loud bone crunching noise.

Chris started beating on a large drum at the end of the hall and in a menacing voice asked, 'Who had access to bricks? Who had a sack to put them in and who disliked Jeff,the baker, so much that they wanted to kill him?'

'Maybe it was Mistress Priscilla who felt he had sold her inferior bread. Or could it have been Oliver Pike who suspected Jeff was dallying with his wife?'

People looked around scrutinising name badges, trying to identify a suspect, someone they could blame for this crime.

When the body had been removed the revellers began to make their way to the dining room where the food was waiting, steaming hot and smelling delicious.

Maddie noticed the strangers and started to walk towards them, eager to find out who they were.

She realised their identity badges varied slightly from those her father had been making all week .The writing, though similar, was smaller, and slanted slightly to the right.

She needed to be nearer to see what names and roles they had been given for the evening, or had they chosen their identities for themselves?

Was she looking at seven new recruits or a group of total strangers, dressed in authentic looking 17th century costumes? Strangers who had gate- crashed their banquet!

They certainly didn't seem to want to talk to anyone.

Suddenly there was a loud scream and the youngest member of this unknown group, fell to the floor. Those standing nearby started to look around for the killer amongst them, but there was nobody near the girl.

In the distance a drum could be heard beating.

Maddie, who was standing close to the body turned to her aunt and said, 'Dad and Uncle Donald have excelled themselves, that body actually looks as if it is bleeding.'

Alice nodded, 'Yes it certainly is realistic.'

Suddenly Chris appeared looking bewildered.

'I don't know who's organised this 'murder'. It's not part of our script, someone is obviously playing a practical joke,' he said.

People started moving towards the dining room again but Maddie was rooted to the spot.

'Dad,' she called. 'Dad, come here.'

Chris walked over to her and looked at the motionless girl on the floor.

'Who is she?' queried Maddie, 'and what has happened to her? It looks as though she has really been injured.'

Chris knelt down and put his hand on the girl's body.

'Oh my God," he whispered, "THAT is real blood, look at my fingers, and I can't feel a pulse. I think she's dead!'

He led Maddie into the kitchen.

'I'll call the ambulance. Go and sit with your grandmother. DO NOT say anything to her or anyone else about what we have discovered and tell Uncle Donald, he's dressed as a monk, I need him here right now.'

Chris left her and rushed back into the hallway.

The area was empty, completely empty.

What on earth was happening? He hadn't been away for more than three minutes and a girl he had never seen before tonight , who had had real blood pumping out of her body had simply vanished.

There was no body, no trace of blood on the floor and he suddenly realised the blood stain on his hand had disappeared as well.

'Someone has somehow played a trick on us,' he said, explaining to Donald what had happened.

'She's just vanished. The body has completely vanished, and the blood as well. I have no idea who she is. She came with those people I didn't recognise but why would total strangers want to pull a stunt like that at our banquet?'

'The strangest thing is they didn't stay around to watch our reaction to their trick, or to make sure she came to no real harm.'

Donald and Chris returned to the dining room.

'Can you see the interlopers?' asked Donald.

Chris glanced around the room at the members of his regiment, all tucking into the various 17th century delicacies as they drank ale and noisily discussed the recent killings, trying to decide who the was the suspect murderer.

All the seats but one were occupied
and Chris and Donald could identify
every single man, woman and child.

'They aren't here,' Chris murmured.'
'This gets weirder by the minute.'
* * * * *

Suddenly the mirror turned black, as
black as a starless night. Chris and I
both gasped in astonishment. Was that
the end?

But almost at once the darkness
cleared.
* * * * *

A young girl, resembling the one who we
had just seen lying on the floor, was
walking towards the kitchen.

As she opened the kitchen door there
was a scene of chaos. Some Roundhead
soldiers were in there looting the place
grabbing wine, beer and any food they
could find.

The girl turned away shouting as she
went to alert the guards on the
battlements, but she was not quick
enough. One of the roundhead soldiers
drew his sword, caught hold of her and
plunged the weapon into her side. She
fell, blood oozing onto the floor around
her body.

Then the murderer, and his fellow
Roundheads, carrying their haul of food

and drink, fled from the kitchen before the breathless guards arrived.

One of the soldiers had stopped in the hallway to beat the Siege drum to awaken the rest of the household.

* * * * *

The scene faded and the mirror darkened again for a split second.

* * * * *

Chris walked over to his mother.

'Did you find out any information about the new recruits,' he asked casually.

Joan's eyes gleamed with pleasure as she answered.

'The first time I spoke to them the adults were very rude and ignored me so then I cleverly cornered one of the children and asked for their names. The young lad told me they were Decornervilles. His name is William and he is here with his parents, his uncle and aunt, his sister and a maid servant called Mary. I think she was the one who just pretended to die.'

"You're better than Miss Marple," he praised Joan and went back to Donald.

His brother in law turned quite white as Chris recounted what Joan had just told him.

'The Decornervilles were Royalist who lived here at Clampet Castle during the Civil War,' Donald explained.

'Life was hard for those imprisoned within the castle but also for those camped outside. During the siege the castle was defended by a small troop of Royalists. They patrolled the battlements during the day keeping watch on the enemy camped outside the walls. At night some men were stationed on the ramparts but the nights were dark and one can only suppose they often fell asleep.'

'One night some drunken Roundheads climbed over a low part of the wall in an attempt to break the siege by stealing all the food and drink they could find, leaving the inhabitants little choice but to surrender.'

'Luckily a Royalist soldier had spotted them and rushed to beat the Siege Drum, to alert everyone in the castle and let them know the wall had been breached.'

'The intruders were shot'

'Sir Percival kept a diary and that event was recorded in it as was the murder of a young maid who had been near the dining room when the Roundheads entered the castle.'

'Her bleeding, lifeless body was found in the hallway, just outside the dining door, where this incident has just occurred.'

Now it was Chris who turned pale.

'That empty seat must belong to Pete Devereux,' he said.

'We must find him. He's a distant descendant of that enemy of the King, Colonel Nicholas Devereux. Pete's the only one here tonight to have come from a family with Roundhead sympathies.'

'We need to protect him as I'm afraid someone from the past may wish to harm him for a crime *he* never committed.'

'Tell Maddie I need her,' he ordered, 'and insist Mother stays with Alice. We can do without her interference just now and she must NEVER know Maddie's secret.'

Donald found his niece and explained what was happening as they ran to the kitchen.

Immediately Maddie began to sort through the herbs that were displayed hanging from the ceiling and the spices on the shelves. She chanted strange sounding words as she chopped and mixed them together.

Pausing in her work she cast some of the mixture into the air shouting, 'Where is the evil? Where is it?'

She spun round and round with her arm outstretched.

'Quick to the north tower,' she instructed the men, as she stopped spinning and realised her arm was pointing in that direction.

Grabbing candles they ran to the tower and began to climb the winding stairs. In a small room at the top they discovered Pete, surrounded by six angry strangers. They seemed but shadows of their former selves, no longer looking human.

They were snarling and rearing up over Pete's cowering body. Unintelligible sounds issued from their lips and there was a terrible smell of death and decay.

Maddie stepped closer and as the apparitions turned to face her she threw her magic mixture towards them. When it touched their translucent bodies they roared and writhed in agony before finally disappearing.

The energy in the tower changed as sweet perfume and a shaft of moonlight filtered into the room.

They all returned to the banquet where an irate Joan confronted them.

'I think those ill-mannered intruders have left without saying thank you, or goodbye,' she stormed. "You must refuse their membership.'

She turned and recognising her son-in-law, asked indignantly, 'What might I ask are you doing here?'

'Rest assured Mother those people will never darken our banquets again,' said Chris winking at his sister, 'and as for Donald? He's here to dance the night away with Alice!'
* * * * *

The images disappeared and Chris, looking visibly shaken, shook his head.

I'll have to make a decision, he said. 'Donald and I have worked hard preparing for this murder mystery evening. I think we either need to change the venue or else remove Pete Devereux from the guest list. That would be the easiest as we know exactly where and how the murders would happen at castle. We would have to rewrite the whole evening if we changed venues.'

He paid me and left, still undecided about what to do.

He contacted me after the banquet to say That despite all the extra work it involved they had in fact decided to switch the venue and the regiment held it's Halloween banquet in an 18th century stately home. The evening was a great success and Pete Devereux had enjoyed himself so much he had asked if he could borrow the scripts to use at the next Devereux regimental banquet, which would not be held at Clampet Castle!

I also received an enormous bouquet of flowers from Mr. Devereux himself.

Carrie Bristol confessed to me that she trusted no one.

'I suspect everyman I meet of lying to me which as you can imagine makes all my relationships very short lived. I don't even believe half of what my girl friends tell me and,' she laughed, 'I often doubt the words that come out my own mouth'

'I was wondering if I was a very gullible person in a previous life and that is why I am so suspicious of everyone and everything they say.'

The mirror was eager to tell her story, showing us a picture of an elegant drawing room as soon as we sat down.

* * * * *

THE SECRET

His latest portrait of me had pride of place over the mantelpiece. Visitors said their eyes were drawn to it as they entered the room and they found it impossible not to keep glancing at that particular picture. Such was the hypnotic power within all the images of me that Joshua Miller painted.

These same visitors were always keen to know if the gossip about my humble beginnings was true and I was happy to entertain them by recounting the story of how we met.

I was just sixteen years old, selling flowers near the Ten Bells Pub in Whitechapel,'I'd explain.

In fact it was spring and I was holding several bunches of daffodils when he passed by.

He looked rich so I held my flowers out towards him, hoping he would stop and buy some, but he seemed uninterested and walked on.

Suddenly he turned, retraced his steps and stopped in front of me. He began studying my face.

'How old are you?' he asked.

'What's that to you Mister?'I replied, giving him a cheeky smile.

'You have such wonderful bone structure,' he said.

I remember thinking, 'Blimey we've got a crazy one here,' but I said nothing as he continued to gaze at my face.

He made a bow and said, 'I'm an artist and I'd like you to accompany me to my studio in Mile End Road so I can paint you. I will purchase all of your flowers if you would do me this honour.'

Now, as you can imagine, this was a really tempting offer. Getting rid of all my flowers so early in the day with the prospect of an afternoon sheltered from the chilly wind and maybe the added bonus of something to eat and drink.

'The price has just gone up,' I said boldly,

'They'll cost you 'alf a guinea.'

'He handed me a coin and took the flowers from my hand.'

'Follow me,' he instructed.

'Wait,' I shouted as he started walking away.

I ran across the street and told my friend, Ali, what was happening.

'Please tell Bert I might be late tonight as I'm off with the toff up the Mile End Road.'

Ali nodded as I patted his dancing bear's muzzle. Then I turned away and hurried after the gentleman.

We walked in silence through the narrow, overcrowded, smelly streets. He seemed anxious to get to his studio.

I waved at those I knew to reassure them I was alright. I didn't want them to worry when they saw a well dressed man carrying my daffodils, and me two or three steps behind, struggling to keep up with him.

We looked out for each other in Whitechapel during those days as many people feared the Ripper was still around, searching for his next victim.

I followed the artist for about twenty minutes until he stopped outside a green door, opened it and ushered me inside.

He settled me in a rocking chair, handed me my daffodils and then he disappeared behind his easel.

When I fidgeted he coughed and when I sat still he narrowed his eyes, looking alternatively at me and then back at his work. I was getting bored and the tingling in my hands was moving up my arms. I needed to move. I lifted my little finger off my knee, just a small movement but he coughed again and said, 'Please don't move.'

After about two hours I got up put down the flowers and said, 'Time's up Mister.'

'I've not finished,' he said, 'would you return tomorrow so I can continue?'

'Cost you double,' I said. 'Money up front.'

Certainly,' he replied and handed me the coins

Over the coming months Joshua sought me out two or three times a week. He always fed me, occasionally bought me a new garment or a trinket and gradually started to correct the way I spoke,

I continually increased the price I charged him and he always paid the sum requested.

I bought new outfits for Bert and even purchased a tiny felt coat for the monkey that sat on his barrel organ.

Life was improving! We ate every night, had wood for the fire and enjoyed a drink or two at our local several times a week.

Friends congratulated us on the change in our fortune, though I suspect many wondered what I really did to earn my pay.

When Ali took me to one side and said, 'Be careful The Ripper is still at large. I've heard some say it could be a toff like that painter you go off with.' I shook my head and replied. 'Na, it's not him. He doesn't even kill spiders.'

Besides, I knew what I knew!

Then one week, which stretched to two and then three, Joshua didn't appear.

Amy Wistley was regularly selling her flowers on my old spot near the Ten Bells pub and Bert and I felt the pangs of hunger once more.

I was desperate and took to walking the dismal, unsanitary streets of Whitechapel, searching for customers as I called out the price of my roses.

During the first week of July 1889 Joshua reappeared, rushing along the street, looking frantically from side to side, searching every face he passed.

There was a look of pure relief when he spotted me, but I pretended indifference and looked away as he approached.

'Lila,' he called.

I took no notice, though I was aware he had moved closer to me.

'Lila, I have amazing news. Do you remember that first portrait I did of you standing in front of the pub. The one where everything was black and white, except for those flowers, which I painted yellow?'

I nodded. It was my favourite.

I've sold it for....,' and he whispered a price in my ear that made me gasp in astonishment.

Apparently, Lord Peter Stanfield, who owned a castle in Scotland, had called at Josh's studio intending to buy a painting for his wife. He'd been so impressed with the pictures he saw that he'd immediately asked Joshua to pack up some of his work and accompany him back up north so his wife could choose her favourite.

He had paid a staggering amount of money for that first portrait of me. The one Josh had called, 'A waif with flowers.'

'Tonight we celebrate,' Josh shouted, wrapping his arms around me and twirling me off my feet.

I am sure you can guess the rest of my story. Joshua's work was sought after. He grew rich and my face became famous. We fell in love, married and moved west into the centre of London.

Of course I return to Whitechapel at least once a week. I have to. When you know what I know and know who I know there is no option.

Despite my silken clothes, palatial house and refined way of speaking I know my roots, After all I'm still a Whitechapel girl at heart.

Besides, there was someone there who I loved even more than Joshua. Someone I had protected during the dark days of 1888 when every man was a suspect and almost every woman went about in fear. Someone, who still needed my protection and always would.

I'd told stories to protect him in the past and I'd told a lie to Joshua on the day I married him. I allowed spinster of this parish to be written on our wedding certificate because I had a secret that I could never tell anyone.

* * * * *

'I need to go away and think,' Carrie said.

'I am guessing I was one of the main characters in that scenario we have just seen, but I've no idea which one?

'Was I Bert who it seems the lies were being told about, Lila who told the lies or Joshua who was ignorant of all the lies his wife was telling?'

It didn't seem to occur to her that she might have actually have been the infamous, Jack The Ripper, which was my first thought, but I kept that idea to myself!

Carrie left and I have no idea if she came to any conclusion about her past life character.

THE DREAMER

My next client had spoken to me on the phone describing a recurrent dream she was experiencing.

'I know mermaids are fictional characters but recently I have been dreaming that I am a mermaid, swimming in a blue sea.'

'It is so real,' she said,

'When I wake I have to look under the duvet to check I still have legs and not the shimmering, scale covered tail I possess while I sleep, but it's never there, just my two useless, withered legs.'

'It's not a nightmare. I love the freedom I have when moving through the water, and I feel so at home surrounded by waving seaweed, coral, fish and fantastic shaped shells. There are other mermaids and mermen too swimming around with me.'

'I have heard so much about you and wondered if a past life regression would help explain my dream.'

Jessie positioned her wheel chair so she was facing the mirror and I sat next

80

to her, both of us, I am sure, were wondering if a past life session could actually explain her dreams.

Personally, I thought it was wishful thinking on her part to have freedom of movement, something she lacked during her waking hours.

* * * * *

THE MERMAID

The mirror turned bright blue, the vibrant colour dazzled us both, and then gradually a horizon appeared separating the deep blue of the sea from the lighter colour of the sky.

Rocky islands appeared, some covered with a reddish seaweed.

There were human like figures sitting on the rocks, but on closer examination we could see that each one had a fish like tail instead of legs.

These beautiful creatures were singing. It was a truly heavenly sound.

The singing faded and one of the mermaids began to speak.

'The words of our songs come from a far distant star called Perchonia. They warn of danger to all species on Planet Earth. It has taken many, many light years, travelling through the Universe, for these melodies to reach us here on earth.'

We, Merpeople, have distant relations living on that planet. Like us they live in a sea, but their water is clear and clean. They have no beings there who have limbs instead of a tail and who pollute their life-sustaining water.

Those on Planet earth who are in tune with us will understand our songs and worry about their future. Sadly most of those who regard earth as their home will continue to destroy their environment.

One of our relations has sent the following message.

'Some of us are going to leave our paradise. We have allies on nearby stars who have perfected the art of intergalactic travel. They have promised that before total extinction strikes those on the earth they will transport us to the stricken planet in the hope that we can influence our distant kin and ensure the survival of their environment.

So we can move among the indigenous population, without detection, they will help us modify our bodies so we have two legs instead of a tail.'

You are listening to a message you, yourself sent from your home star, Perchonia, many light years ago. You dispatched it so it would arrive at a time when it would be expedient for you to listen to the words and try to help your present homeland from destruction.'

* * * * *

'Im guessing they didn't get the modification of the tail quite right for me,' she smiled and looked down at her immobile legs.

'Thank you what we have just seen has explained a lot for me.'

'I have a degree in marine conservation. I had no idea why I chose that subject. I'd planned to study history so I went to look round that department at Plymouth University, but when I discovered they did the conservation course I applied for that instead.'

'It all makes sense now as to why I did that, and I have recently been offered a research post studying the effects of micro plastic in the English Channel.'

'I start next month.'

Jessie wheeled herself out with a big smile on her face.

'From now on I shall enjoy my dreams,' she said.

I sat in my cubicle, delighted that Jessie had been so happy and positive when she left. I still didn't understand how the mirror worked but the results were pleasing many people.

I looked towards it and suddenly image appeared, an image that I instantly knew was me in a previous life.

* * * * *

THE SPY

To spy or not to spy, that was the question running through my mind as I turned into Moorcroft lane.

Grandmother had been quite explicit when explaining the risks involved in the adventure she wanted me to undertake, but she had spelled out the benefits too.

'I have a secret to tell you,' she whispered to me just hours before she died.

'The only person you can ever tell is your first born female grandchild.'

I listened with amazement, not sure if my grandmother was hallucinating.

Since her death, two months ago I have strolled along this lane several times, looking for a vantage point where I could part the undergrowth and see the field in front of the ruined castle. I never stopped as I didn't want to draw attention to myself.

If anyone had seen me walking along the lane I am sure they would have presumed I was heading for nearby Loxton, not reconnoitring spying places.

I needed to find a suitable spot before the next full moon and before the brambles, nettles and bracken produced new growth in spring forming an impenetrable barrier.

I pinpointed a location where I could cross the roadside ditch and hide behind some sapling oaks. Here I would be completely hidden from the lane and concealed by dead bracken from anyone or anything in the nearby field.

One Saturday night in March I lay in bed listening to my sister snoring softly beside me and after I was sure my parents were also asleep I slipped out of bed, got dressed and wrapping my fur lined cloak around my body I stole down the stairs and out of the house.

I needed no lantern as the moon was shining, lighting up the way to my chosen spot in Moorcroft Lane.

As I jumped over the ditch and pushed my way through the head-high fronds of dead bracken, a cloud obscured the moon and in the shadow of those sapling oaks I waited for my eyes to become accustomed to the darkness of the evening sky.

I knew I would have to be patient and keep very still.

Suddenly I saw a something moving silently across the field. I gasped in amazement.

So Grandmother's story was true!

As the shape glided nearer I could see it was composed of many small bodies and some of them were carrying tiny orbs of light.

I hardly dare to breathe least I be discovered for then I knew I would be cursed for the rest of my life.

The moon slipped from behind the cloud and illuminated the fairy rings in the grass. Now I could see quite clearly the colourful costumes the tiny figures were wearing and their shimmering transparent wings.

I stood still. I knew I couldn't risk moving a muscle for fear of revealing myself.

I heard music, a beautiful lilting melody, and the tiny figures began to dance, weaving in and out of the dark green circles in the grass.

I also heard high pitched voices, some were talking and others were singing.

I couldn't understand the words and yet I knew instinctively these little creatures were happy as they danced and played their music under the light of the full moon.

Remembering Grandmother's warning I fought against the overwhelming urge to join them.

I heard a rustling sound behind me and glanced over my shoulder. My sister, Anna, was standing watching the activity in the field.

Slowly I held up my hand, entreating her to keep still and silent but she had a strange glazed expression on her face and to my horror she stepped forward and started to walk towards the little people.

Instantly all activity stopped and as the moon disappeared once more behind a cloud these magical beings spread their wings and drifted up into the starlit sky, taking my sister with them.

I was alone in the hedgerow.

I shook my head, surely I had dreamt seeing Anna. I went home truly expecting to find my sister asleep in our bed, but the room was empty.

Naturally my parents were concerned when Anna could not be found in the morning. They asked me if I had heard her moving around in the night.

Remembering again grandmother's warning about what the fairies could do to anyone revealing their whereabouts I answered honestly, 'No, I never heard her get out of bed last night.'

I went back to spy on that field many times when there was a full moon. Sometimes the fairies were there, but usually the field was empty.

I never saw my sister again.

Now I have a secret to pass on, many years hence, to Alice May, my first granddaughter who was born yesterday.

* * * * *

I looked down at my mug of coffee, it was still on my lap. I had been so engrossed in what the mirror was showing me I had quite forgotten to drink it.

Quickly I grabbed a pen and some paper, anxious to write down all I had seen and heard before my next client arrived.

Later that night I searched for Loxton on the internet. It had existed as a village in the 19th century but has now been incorporated into the nearby town of Greasham.

Apparently some owners of property built near the ruined castle have reported strange happenings when there is a full moon. Some have seen flashing lights, others heard singing and many say the area is haunted by a young girl called Anna who disappeared without trace one moonlit night in March 1862.

Why I was suddenly shown this story? I have no idea, but I do believe fairies exist and I am sure that the girl who watched them that moonlit night was me. I intend to take a day off soon and go and visit the area near the ruined castle in Greasham.

I also believe I can look forward to having a granddaughter called Alice May.

THE GIFTED SESSION

My next client was an elderly gentleman. His daughter had gifted him a past life regression session.

'He has this strange desire to collect creepy looking stone statues and watering cans,' she informed me."

'He must have at least two hundred in his back garden and the whole family would love to know if there is a reason from a past life why he collects these unusual items.'

'The stone figures frighten me, they are standing among the bushes as though they are hiding, just waiting to pounce on you as you walk by. '
'Even Bonzo his dog doesn't like them. He growls and lifts his legs as he passes each one'.
'I've tried to interest my father in some modern metal figures and garden ornaments but he's not interested, he just wants ancient stone figures and watering cans of all shapes and sizes.'

THE COLLECTOR-
Mr Hudson arrived as I was finishing my coffee.
'Can I tell you something while you finish your drink?' he asked.
'Certainly,' I replied.
'I write novels under the pseudonym Peter Craven- Smyth,' he said.
'You may have heard of me and the truth is I have a secret. Those stone men and women my daughter hates so much give me inspiration for the books I write
Those modern metal or moulded ones, she's always encouraging me to buy, have no personalities but the ones carved from a block of stone speak to me in a way I can understand and I fashion my tales around them.'

'I know the children were frightened of them when they were small and even now they find them quite intimidating so I've never confessed that I listen to those 'people' as they tell me their stories.'

'Let's keep that a secret between the two of us shall we?' he said and I nodded in agreement.

'As for the watering cans, I have no idea why I feel the need to buy so many,' he laughed. 'I never use them as I have a long hose pipe that reaches all round the garden.'

'My daughter probably told you the whole family think I'm crazy.'

'Well let's see if a past life regression can throw some light on it,' I suggested as we sat facing the mirror.

Nothing happened. The reflection of my rainbow curtains was all we could see.

So we took the conventional route and I regressed him over the Bridge of time to a past life. I recorded his answers to the questions I asked and this is what he described to me.

* * * * *

He stepped off that bridge into a field in China. He was a young boy, one of six children, and like his older siblings, he had been assigned a task to do each day.

His job was to carry a yoke with a pail at either end, past the flooded paddy fields, to a nearby river, fill the buckets, and then take them back to the family home.

The round trip took him nearly two hours.

One day he stopped and looked at all the water in the paddy field.

'Water is water,' he said to himself and bent down to fill his buckets from the ditch.

It was too soon to go back home so he took the yoke off his shoulder and sat by the rice field dreaming of the day when he could pass this task onto his younger brother.

'If only we had some sort of container to hold the water,' he thought. 'I could go to the river twice every other day and on the days when my mother was using the stored water I could have a rest from this journey, maybe go fishing with my father and the older boys, or help my sisters weed the paddy fields. That would be easier than carrying these pails to and fro every single day.'

Unfortunately, he couldn't think of how the water could be stored in a way that wouldn't stop the hot sun drying it up.

He watched the sun move across the sky and when he judged an appropriate amount of time had passed for him to have been to the river and back he picked up his yoke, rested it on his shoulder and returned home.

His mother used some of the water to make soup for the evening meal.

During that night the boy woke up with pains in his stomach and so did all the other members of his family.

Even though he was ill he had to fetch water for the family the next day. He stopped by the paddy field.

He was tempted to fill his pails from here again, but then he thought, 'We have soup most days and we are never ill. What if it was the water I collected yesterday that made us so sick?'

He walked onto the river.

Sadly two days later his younger brother died of dysentery.

The boy never filled his pails from the paddy fields again and he never told anyone what he had done.

Now he didn't have a younger brother to take over the job of collecting water. So day after day he had to walk past the paddy fields to the river, all the while dreaming about inventing a container that would store water and save him his daily trek.

* * * * *

Mr Hudson was weeping when the session ended. I realised straight away why the mirror had not shown us this tale. He would have been even more upset if he had seen the action played out in front of him.

'I'm guessing some part of me remembers what I did and how my action resulted in my brother dying and may be in a strange way I see watering cans as the answer to my water storage idea.' he said.

'Bit bizarre really as they are for pouring water, not storing it.'

He stood up to leave and as he was shaking my hand I saw colours out of the corner of my eye. The reflection of my rainbow drapes was fading and being replaced by an image of a desert. As a chilly breeze blew through my unit I quickly motioned for Mr Hudson to turn round and sit down again.

* * * * *

A small woman wearing a loose black robe and with her head covered was standing near some rocks. She had some cloths in her hand and a skin bucket was on the sand by her feet.

As we watched, the sky began to lighten and the woman started to turn over nearby rocks.

Their exposure to the cool early morning air caused water droplets to form on the rocks. As the sun rose above the horizon we could see the tiny droplet of dew.

One by one the woman quickly covered the rocks with bits of her material. Once they had soaked up the water she began to wring out the cloths allowing the water to drip into her skin bucket.

She continued to do this task until her bucket was full.

She made her way back to a collection of tents. The sun was beating down on her and the sand and her progress was slow.

There were some small cups on the ground near a fire. The woman lifted her bucket and started to pour water from it into them. Even though she was careful some of her precious load missed the cup, quickly disappearing into the sand.

The woman stood shaking her head and sighing as the image slowly faded from our view.

* * * * *

Mr. Hudson looked thoughtful.

'Seems like I have been responsible for collecting water in more than one life, and each time the equipment hasn't been satisfactory'.

'A watering can, could certainly have made it easier to pour the liquid from a bucket into a cup and can be used to store water but isn't an ideal vessel for carrying water a great distance. I mean they still use yokes to carry items around in China today.'

'What an entertaining afternoon. I shall ponder on what I've seem while contemplating my collection of watering cans.'

He stood up again, shook my hand and left.

THE CONNECTION

Kevin came to see if any of my sessions would help him understand something that had happened recently. Through a mutual friend he had been introduced to a lady called Beth and they had both felt an instant connection drawing them together.

They had certainly never met before during this life and knew nothing about each other, but they both felt there was something that linked them together.

'I can only think we met in a previous life,' he said.

'I've suggested that theory to Beth.

She says that is all rubbish but it is the only explanation I can think of so my question is, 'If I did meet her in the past can you regress me to that specific lifetime?'

I wasn't convinced the mirror had the power to direct him to a definite lifetime so we agreed to try the conventional method of past life regression.

I decided I would relax him and lead him to a tower. Inside there would be many doors each one leading to a past life and I would ask him to choose a door which would take him back to a time when he had met someone he had been lucky enough to meet again in this lifetime.

To my surprise as we sat talking in front of my mirror I felt a cool damp wind blowing around me and the mirror turned misty.

* * * * *

THE TWINS

A young woman was lying in bed, holding a baby in each arm She looked pale and very tired.

'Will you look at what we have here,' she said to the children standing beside the bed.

'Not one baby but two so you have each got your wish as one's a boy and this one's a girl.

'What shall we call the babes, Mammy?' asked the smallest child.

'I'm thinking Fergus and Siobhan, but we'll see what your Da thinks when he gets in. He'll be as surprised as I am to see that not one but two babes have arrived.'

When he eventually arrived home Jo O'Hara was not well pleased when he realised there would be an extra female mouth to feed in future, but he was truly gladdened to discover he had another son, who in years to come could help with the heavy work on their small holding.

The babies thrived and as they grew older three more babies were born into the family.

Now there were now nine mouths to feed and with only the crops from their small holding, milk from their cow and eggs from their hens they ate a very restricted diet.

There was always a pot of potato soup simmering on the hob. Boiled potatoes in their skins and moistened with buttermilk was a staple breakfast food for the family

In summer onions and leeks were harvested from the garden and they added flavour to the lunchtime mash.

The O'Hara family rarely ate the eggs their hens produced as these were taken to the local market each week and sold to get some money for the rent, or used to swop for strips of bacon to enrich the soup.

When times were hard these goods were even taken by the rent collector in lieu of money.

Everyone in the family had a job to do and when they were young the twins were in charge of feeding the hens and collecting the eggs every morning and again in the evening before they went to bed.

They spent every possible minute with each other and felt no need to play with their siblings.

In 1845 the father came home one night and told his wife that he had noticed brownish freckles on some of the potato leaves.

'Jacko Marsh has the same problem and Timmy O'keefe too. They say it's a blight,' he explained, "and we need to start harvesting as soon as possible to stop the tubers decaying.'

The next day the whole family went into the field. The eldest girl was put in charge of the babies. While Fergus, his father and big brother dug trenches in the potato field, Siobhan and her mother followed behind carrying sacks to collect the potatoes in. Most of the tubers were fine but some had developed those sinister dark patches.

'Put those in a separate sack,' ordered Siobhan's mother and leave the ones that have turned soggy with the disease where you find them.

That year and the next they managed to harvest enough potatoes to last them a full year and even save some as seed potatoes to be planted in 1847.

They called that year 'Black 47' as everything seemed to go wrong. The diseased tubers left in the soil had contaminated it and most of the potato plants were blighted. There were not many healthy tubers to harvest.

The absentee landlord increased their rent and his lackey refused to take eggs or produce instead of money. There was little food in the local market to batter for with eggs, as grain and other commodities were being sent to England. So the family killed and ate their hens.

The father and his eldest son occasionally found labouring jobs to do and the twins spent most of their days foraging around the countryside for berries, nettles and mushrooms which their mother added to the watery soup she made each day.

The landlord's agent threatened them with eviction.

Having watched their neighbour being turned out of his home, a hut made of mud and sods, and then seeing the agent set it on fire so the family could not return, the twin's parents decided to sell their cow so they could pay the rent.

Times were really hard that winter and the family were always hungry. Occasionally Jo caught a rabbit in one of his traps and Fergus sometimes killed a bird with his slingshot.

The mother was weak as she had been eating sparingly, giving her portion to her starving children. One by one the babies became ill and died and a week later the mother did too.

The quarterly rent was due. If they didn't pay it they would be evicted and have to go to the workhouse.

The twins were distraught. They had heard tales of the workhouse. Males and females lived in separate quarters and were not allowed to fraternise. They had never been separated from each other and begged their father to pay the rent.

Patiently he explained the situation to them. If they paid the rent with the money left from the sale of the cow they could live in their home for the next three months, but they would have no food to eat and with nothing else left to sell there would be no money for the next instalment of rent.

It was inevitable they would at some point end up in the workhouse where they would at least have a roof over their heads and food to eat.

Instead of paying the landlord it was decided that the remaining money from the sale of the cow would be used to pay for the eldest son to go to Liverpool. It was hoped he would find a job and be able to send some of his pay back to the stricken family.

But before he left and just three days before the rent was due a neighbour came with some news.

A boat had docked in the nearby harbour and was unloading its cargo. The holds would be empty on the return trip and the captain was offering a free passage for any young men who would work on the boat during the return trip. Hopefully they would find jobs once the boat arrived back in Canada.

The father took Fergus outside and convinced him that he should take this opportunity of a new life and leave with his elder brother.

'I can't leave Siobhan,' Fergus cried.

'Son,' said the father, 'in three days we will be evicted. You are 14 years old and have worked all your life on the land but once we are in the workhouse they will make you work for your food, most likely in a factory or down a mine and I can tell you now neither will be a pleasant occupation.'

'You will not see your sister everyday as you do now but there are opportunities in a country like Canada, opportunities that will enable you to earn money and pay for her passage to join you.'

'Son I am not asking you to go I am ordering you to leave, with your brother tonight, while your sister sleeps.'

With a heavy heart Fergus did as he was told.

The father felt it was too cruel to tell his daughter the truth and so he explained to Siobhan the next morning that Fergus had heard of some work nearby and had left at once to try and secure a job. There had been no time to wake her to say goodbye, and if he did not get the job he would join them in the workhouse.

She was heartbroken.

The family packed up what few possessions they owned and waited for the rent collector to arrive. Finding out they could not pay they were ordered out of the hovel.

The workhouse was overcrowded. The work was hard and the food was inadequate. Sanitary arrangements were poor and many of the evicted men, women and children died in there, including the twin's father.

Siobhan and her sister were luckier than some of the other young women living in the work house, as they were offered the chance to go to Australia to become serving wenches.

Siobhan was unsure what to do. There had been no news from Fergus. She hoped he was happy in his new job, and waited patiently for him to visit her, but as he never did she decided to leave with her sister.

The journey was long but the girls were well fed on board that ship. Sadly when they reached Australia the sisters were sent to work for families that lived many miles apart and they lost contact with each other.

Fergus and his brother found work in Canada. The letters they wrote home never reached their sisters who were now in Australia, so they never received any replies.

Sadly the twins were never reunited in that life.

* * * * *

Both Kevin and I were in tears when the mirror misted over. Tears of sadness for that poor family and all the others who had suffered during the potato famine, but our tears were mingled with a feeling of happiness as surely Fergus and Siobhan, now reincarnated as Beth and Kevin, had finally been reunited.

THE HORROR STORY
I really didn't believe the mirror would ever show a horrific story but I was wrong.

My next client Holly was a teenager. Her mother had spoken to me the week before saying her daughter had problems which were not being resolved by the health service and she wanted to see if showing her daughter what life was like for her in future could in fact shock her and make her stop her destructive behaviour.

I was not at all happy to try this but the mother forwarded me a letter from Holly's consultant saying he was in favour of us trying a future life progression with her.

It was a hot day when Holly arrived. She was wearing a long sleeved jumper and had a scarf around her neck. I asked her if she wanted to take off her jumper before we started but she was adamant that she was ok and just wanted to get started.

WARNING- Holly's story is rather upsetting.

The mirror went cloudy and a surprising scene unfolded in front of us

* * * * *

THE BAD BLOOD

An elderly woman was standing by the side of a fast flowing river. She was wearing a black cloak and was surrounded by a group of men dressed in tunics and stockings.

Nearby a group of women were pointing their fingers at the woman and chanting, 'Bad blood, bad blood, bad blood."

Two of the men took hold of the woman and with great force threw her into the river. Within seconds she disappeared under the water.

* * * * *

The mirror went cloudy just for a minute or two as we sat in silence. When it cleared we saw Holly's reflection in it.

Although I was sitting beside her in my cubicle there was no sign of me in that mirror.

Holly's image began to speak.

* * * * *

I, Holly, know what I know about the bad blood inside me because of that dream I had when I was six years old.

I saw that a long time ago a curse was put on me to make me full of bad blood. A barber surgeon used leaches to try and rid my body of the evil that was in me, but he failed.

The villagers knew about my blood and were frightened of me so they drowned me in the cold dark waters of the river.

I know in this life my blood flows as red as a poppy but within that red river that pours from the cuts on my arm there are dark substances. Substances that could taint the whole planet with evil!

I knew I was safe when I was a child as my body contained a very small amount of blood but as I reached adolescence and my body developed, the volume of blood increased and so did the badness.

That's when I started to release the build up of that sinister liquid.

I trusted Dr. Marshall when I first went to see him and I told him something I had never spoken about before. I told him about my blood. I told him about its badness and how it could affect other people.

I thought he understood but gradually I realised he was like the others, not able to recognise my pain and my fear or help alleviate it in any way apart from offering me bottles of pills and endless sessions of counselling.

I lost faith in him completely when he suggested I could prevent the spread of this evil by never cutting myself again.

'So you want me to keep all this badness inside me forever do you?' I screamed at him.

In fact I screamed so loud and so long that he suggested to my mother that I should stay in an adolescent unit for a week or two. I didn't object. I wondered if there were others there who shared my heritage and if so maybe we would work out a plan to jointly save the Planet from our badness.

I think my mother was surprised and relieved by my cooperation.

When we arrived at the unit I was shown into a room and asked to unpack my bag for the attendant to see what I had brought with me. Naturally I refused. I wasn't going to let them see my' kit' hidden among my clothes.

To my horror the bag was forcibly taken from me and my knives, razor blades and plasters were revealed and confiscated.

I ranted and raved. How would I be able to let the badness out? I couldn't keep it in me. I promised over and over I would collect the blood and hand it to them so they could dispose of it safely and stop it from contaminating others..

I only wished to escape from its horror and at that moment in time had no desire to impose its evil on others.

Dr Marshall was called and tried to calm me down. I ignored him.

Someone stuck a needle in my arm and I slept.

When I awoke a lady I'd never seen before, was sitting by my bed. She asked if I was hungry and I realised I was, so she escorted me to the dining room.

I felt like a prisoner.

There were seven or eight girls in there. Some were eating. Some were sitting looking at the food and others were pushing it around with their knife and fork. No one was talking and no one looked happy.

Although I have always known that others have been programmed with the same curse as me I had never been able to establish contact with them.

'Maybe it's true,' I thought as I glanced around, 'maybe some of them here really are contaminated like me.'

Over the following ten days I was a model inmate. I cooperated with the unit's routine and especially enjoyed mealtimes. The food was good and I used this opportunity to study my fellow prisoners as they sat, several of them refusing to eat. I started to imagine what their starved blood was like.

It felt evil to me.

Slowly I realised the urge to find other afflicted people was growing stronger. I was also becoming aware that my main concern was no longer to save the planet from destruction but to completely rid myself and others of this curse, at whatever cost to humanity.

I knew I needed to formulate a plan of action but as I had no tools to release it, the badness was building up inside me, threatening to engulf me with unbelievable terrors.

Each day the pressure was growing. I was so full of poison I had no room for food in my body.

I sat at the table, copying the others, moving my food from side to side around my plate, heaping it up to expose the porcelain, raising my laden fork to my mouth, allowing nothing to pass between my lips.

Yesterday, the girl sitting opposite me fainted during our evening meal. In the resulting chaos I managed to slip a knife into my trouser pocket. Of course there was an outcry when it was discovered that a piece of cutlery was missing. We were searched, our rooms were turned upside down and everyone was questioned but nothing was found.

No one thought to look inside the cistern behind the toilet!

I knew the knives they let us use were really blunt. Would my hidden treasure be sharp enough to pierce the skin of my fellow victims?

Should I confide in them so they knew I was saving them from total depravity?

We were watched at all times and doors were never locked. How could I distract the ever present supervisors so I could accomplish my mission?

These questions troubled me.

Dr Marshall came daily, worried about my lack of appetite and lethargy. He seemed almost anxious for me to start screaming and shouting again.

I was tired during the day because I lay awake each night monitoring the movements of the staff. They carry out their inspections at regular intervals during darkness and I timed and mentally noted who went where and when.

I feel tonight is when I must act. I have perfected my plan but the build up of that fiendish evil inside me is making me somewhat light headed.

When the assistant passes by, just after midnight, I slip out of bed and walk to the toilet. The light is always on so I can easily see to recover the knife.

I must be silent and I must be quick.

I really want to assist the others. I don't want them to suffer like I do but I am not sure I have the strength to use my weapon on them while my arteries and veins are filled with boiling liquid so I think I must be selfish and help myself first.

The knife isn't cutting my skin. Frantically I saw it back and forth over my wrist, waiting eagerly to see that red river start to flow.

All I can see as I sink to the floor is a cascade of redness arching above my head and then blackness.

* * * * *

Holly sat motionless and silent as her reflection was speaking.

Neither of us spoke for at least three minutes and then Holly gave a long sigh.

'Thank you,' she said and got up to leave.

Six weeks later I heard from her mother. Holly was apparently mortified by the vision she had seen as a possible future for herself.

Having realised the idea of her having 'bad blood' came from a past life it was she who had been instrumental in searching out a therapist who was able to clear the memory from her DNA.

During the last two weeks Holly had not self harmed, had returned to school and even felt confident enough to attended a family barbecue.

'I would like to thank you and your mirror for giving Holly a future,' her mother said.

THE FRIEND
My friend Pat gave me a lift to a meeting last month and in return I promised her a regression session. She came in after work and relaxed in the chair.
* * * * *
THE FLAT EARTH

I've had such fun for the last three nights at the meeting I attended at Ward's Opera House in Brockport.

Who would think that in this year of 1887 there are people who still believed the earth is flat?

M.C Flanders is one such person who firmly believes this is true, and he put up a really convincing case against the two scientists who were equally adamant that the earth is spherical.

I was lucky enough to have received an invite to the debate. Along with four others from this town I had been chosen to vote, for or against Flanders' theory at the end of the third night of the ongoing debate.

I must admit I didn't get much sleep before the last session. So many questions were spiralling through my head.

If I jumped on a boat and set sail would I really at some point during my voyage drop off the edge of the planet? And if so where would I end up?

If indeed the earth was flat what had happened to all those unfortunate souls who had met their end in this way?

Is there a place they go or are they suddenly precipitated into total oblivion?

Does sailing right, I suppose I mean east, end you up at a totally different place than if you head west?

Questions, questions, questions.

I knew I didn't want to make such an expedition to test out Flanders' theories (just in case), but I wanted to be sure of my beliefs before I cast my vote the following night.

Later that week The Brockport Democrat reported that the townsfolk voted unanimously that the earth was flat.

* * * * *

As the mistiness cleared from the mirror Pat was smiling.

'I so hope that is true,' she said. 'I love the idea that I was once so naive as to believe the world was flat.'

She later checked out the name M C Flanders and discovered the meetings we had seen had in fact taken place in March 1887!

THE SEARCH

Lara was 19 and she explained that she had spent her whole life searching for something that she felt she had lost.

'I don't know what it is I'm constantly looking for. In fact I don't even know if it is an object, a person or a place.

It makes me feel quite depressed because if don't know what I have lost how can I ever find it?

The mirror showed her a possible answer to her question.

* * * * *

THE OLD MAN

He wasn't so much a down and out just downtrodden and heartbroken by life itself. He rarely smiled or acknowledged others when they greeted him. Most days he sat in the park huddled up at one corner of a park bench, audibly sighing if anyone dared to sit at the other end.

He always carried a bag of crumbs and nuts which he scattered around his feet and then silently watched the wildlife enjoying their daily treat. The birds came close, they knew he meant them no harm and the squirrels were sometimes brave enough to takes nuts from his hand. He regarded them as the only friends in his troubled life and looked forward to their daily visits. He was certain no human cared if he lived or died.

In autumn he watched the leaves piling up against the tree trunks, litter bins, and the other park benches.

Minute by minute more and more floated gracefully down to earth.

He saw a photographer watching them too, appraising their vibrant colours and capturing their descent in his pictures.

An artist set up his easel nearby and mixed his oils with care, anxious to replicate the exact hue of the autumnal leaves as they drifted round his feet.

He watched people ambling over the crackling carpet underfoot, dogs off their leads chasing the spiralling leaves and the park keeper busy sweeping the leaves into piles all along the pathway.

He observed the activities around him, lost in thought about times long gone.

He remembered sweeping up leaves and burning them on bonfires every 5th November while fireworks lit up the night sky. Happy memories that helped him forget his pains.

He noticed the park keeper retire into his shed.

'Brew time,' he thought.

Two young boys came charging down the cleared pathway. They stopped near the first pile of leaves and one whispered something in the ear of his mate.

They began to kick the leaves high into the air. Moving along the path, and chuckling as they went, destroying all the neat piles as they kicked and threw armfuls of leaves at each other.

Their mothers, deep in conversation and some way behind, were oblivious to their sons' actions.

The park keeper appeared and scratched his head.

'Whatever happened here?' he asked the old man. 'I know there is a breeze but it's not strong enough to cause this chaos.'

The old man shrugged, he was remembering happier times when he and his brother had kicked apart piles of newly swept up leaves. They had done it in this very park, while the park keeper drank his mid morning brew!

In winter he brushed snow from the bench's wooden slats so he could spread out a plastic bag and occupy his regular spot.

He watched snowball fights, children making snowmen and others enjoying rides on sledges.

One day when the daffodils were in bloom he noticed a woman sitting on the next bench. She was watching him and when he caught her eye she smiled. He thought she was looking at the spring flowers so he turned away from her.

She was there the next day and the next. He was suspicious, annoyed and too shy to interact with her.

On the fourth day she was there before him. He had been delayed and in his absence the park keeper had escorted a tree surgeon round the park.

Today as he shambled into the park he stopped in front of a tree. She watched as he gently stroked its trunk, disfigured by age and by the enormous yellow cross painted upon it.

A mark that denoted its destiny.

He sat in his usual place, tears rolling down his face.

She got up, sat next to him and simply took hold of his hand.

Having laboured with wood for nearly sixty years John Legg carpenter and joiner, had calloused, rough and arthritic fingers. It pained him to pick up a mug, tie his shoe laces and even to throw crumbs to the birds.

Dorothy never forgot that first time she held his hand. It was one of those memories locked inside her mind that she treasured and recalled when she thought about him. There were so few memories and each one was precious.

121

From that day onwards they met every morning, a meeting of soulmates. They talked and laughed, held hands and fed the wildlife.

She told him how she had once hated the dark nights of winter.

'Now I draw the curtains, turn up the dimmer switch and adjust the angle poise lamp so it points at the table, then I'm ready for my jigsaw hour,' she said.

'In fact it is usually much longer than an hour that I sit with my puzzle. I tell myself, I'll just put one more bit in, but if I find it quickly I feel cheated and because I don't really want to stop I look for one more piece and then another and another.'

'Sometimes one or two hours go by before I finally stop and go to bed. It keeps my brain busy and staff at the local charity shop supply me with puzzles that have been donated. I do them and if all the bits are there I stick a 'complete' label on the front of the box so customers can be confident there are no bits missing from the puzzle they are buying'

'One year my sister gave me a 4000 piece jigsaw. The picture was of a castle somewhere in Germany. The sky was blue and there were many green trees. Not a picture I would have chosen to do, especially with so many pieces, most of them either green or blue! My sister had obviously bought it, thinking it would keep me busy during the dark nights of winter.

It would be far too big to fit on my jigsaw board, in fact it would take up most of my dining room table, probably for several months.

Then I had a brilliant idea. I placed a postcard in the local newsagents. It said, 'Tuesday night is Jigsaw Night, 7-9p.m. at 4 Grove Place. Come and help complete a 4000 piece jigsaw.'

That was two years ago and four people come regularly each Tuesday. That first one was a real challenge for us all but we did finish it and since then have done many more. I am grateful to my sister as through her I have made new friends and I always look forward to our Tuesday night get together.

He told her about his shelf devoted to hats in the hall cloakroom.

'There's everything in there from a bobble hat to a trilby,' he said.

'Being bald I need to wear a hat as the sun burns my hairless head in summer and the wind freezes it in winter.'

'My son gave me the first hat. It was a woolly bobble hat and he said it would keep me warm when it snowed, and that's very true but when I caught sight of myself wearing it I realised I looked ridiculous. It is a young man's hat, but he meant well and I keep it to remind me of his kindness.'

'Then a neighbour donated his spare panama hat, extolling its virtues for a summer's day and I've worn it once or twice when I've been to watch a cricket match here in the park.'

'I picked up a flat cap for just £3 in the local charity shop, but I've never worn it. When I tried it on at home and saw my reflection in the mirror I thought it made me look a hundred years old, so it's lying on the shelf next to my brother's boater which he used to wear when he performed with a barbershop quartet.'

'I know my trilby is somewhat battered,' he explained, 'but it was my Dad's and it's a hat of memories and that's why I wear it most days.'

She explained that only her parents had ever called her Dorothy.

'It was too much of a mouthful for most people to say and once I started school my friends quickly shortened my name to Dot or Dotty. I hated the latter as soon as I realised its crazy connotations but I was too shy to tell the children to call me Dorothy.'

'The nicknames stuck with me right up until the time I became an aging hippie.'

'Yes I was probably twice the age of most of the flower power people in the 60s but I loved the Kaftans, crushed velvet hot pants and the psychedelic culture they embraced.'

'Someone in the group I hung out with started calling me 'Hippy Dotty' which was quickly changed to Hippy Dippy and some lazy folk even shortened it to HD.'

'I was reminded that Dippy was in fact, like Dotty, a synonym for 'crazy' but I was past caring. From the shy five year old who had acquired a new name when she started school I had morphed into a new me, Hippy Dippy, and I was happy. My friends from that era still call that.'

He told her about his late brother who had worked on steam trains but had never been really happy in his job once

diesel locomotives replaced them in the
60's.

'After his retirement he bought a
cottage with a garden bordering onto a
renovated steam railway line and once a
day an engine with three carriages full of
tourist would chug past his garden. The
drivers knew he would be watching and
when his house came into view they
blew the whistle letting him know they
were on their way.'

'As the passengers, steeped in
nostalgia, sat in carriages with string
luggage racks, photos proclaiming
Skegness to be so bracing and smoke
from the engine drifting past the
windows Bert was always waiting on his
lawn with a tea towel in each hand.

When the train steamed by he waved
his towels, as though they were flags, at
the drivers and the passengers.'

She reminisced about a tree in the
park where she lived when she was
young.

'The locals called it 'The Magpie Tree'
as there was usually at least one magpie
sitting in it when you went by. Some of
the locals spat when they saw a bird and
said 'Morning Mister Magpie,' some
saluted but I counted how many there

were so I could say the poem about them I had learned in school.'

'I hated it when there was only one. I didn't want sorrow in my life and so I would close my eyes and when I opened them and saw it again I pretended it was a different bird so could say 'two for joy.'

'One day I decided to climb the tree and sit next to the two magnificent birds chattering on a low branch. Of course they flew away as soon as I began to climb but I discovered three shiny milk bottle tops and a silver sixpence hidden in crevices of that branch. That was a day of real joy for me.'

He boasted about his appearance on The Antiques Roadshow.

'I took along a pocket watch which I had inherited from my grandfather. It was his pride and joy and he polished it every morning before slipping it into his waistcoat pocket.

'Family heirloom,' he'd say if anyone asked about it. 'Centuries old.'

'We didn't know whether to believe him.'

'So when I saw this programme about antiques on TV, oh it must have been in the late 70s, I thought I'd take it and get it valued by an expert.

127

To say there was excitement when I produced it would be an understatement. I was suddenly surrounded by a group of very excited experts and things were quickly set in motion for the watch and I to have our five minutes of fame.'

'It turned out that Grandfather's watch was something very special. A rare 17th century English Verge in a fine silver and tortoise shell case, made by Michael Johnson, and in an impressive condition.'

'I had thought that maybe it was valuable but after they told me just how many thousands of pounds it was worth I remember muttering, 'I'll never sell it, it's a family heirloom,' and then they had to find a chair for me to sit in and recover from the shock.'

'After my son died there was no family member to inherit it and so I donated it to clock makers section of The Science Museum in London.'

'Just imagine, 'she said one morning as they sat holding hands, 'In three years time we will be able to say that we have lived in two different centuries.'

He didn't reply.

During an early morning hospital appointment, on the day the tree

surgeon visited the park, his doctor had painted an invisible yellow cross on John's body, denoting that he would not live to see in the twenty-first century!
* * * * *

I felt slightly disappointed for Lara because although the session was long and detailed it didn't really give her any clue as to what or who she was searching for.

'All I can think,' she said, 'is that I am looking for someone special I knew in a previous life but maybe we won't be reunited until we are much older.'

THE MOTHER

I'm just interested to see if I have lived before,' Jill said, when she booked the appointment.
* * * * *

THE POTION

The apothecary picked up the balance with his left hand. The weights, tiny slithers of metal, dragged down the left hand dish of the scales. Carefully he scrutinised each ingredient before picking it up with his bone scoop and adding it to the right hand dish.

She watched as slowly, as if by magic, the left hand container rose and the right hand one descended. When they were balanced and all movement stopped, the apothecary tipped the mixture into a paper cone and handed it to her. In return she slipped her precious guilder out of her pocket and into his outstretched hand.

She opened the door to his house and looked around. There was no one about to see her leaving.

Walking home, along the dike she had her fingers crossed, hoping that she had not wasted her precious coin on this evil looking powder.

She never forgot the smell and the taste of that mixture. No words could describe how awful it was, but she persevered and followed the apothecary's instructions. 'A pinch to be taken in water, morning and evening, for 15 days.'

She smiled, it had certainly been worth all the discomfort. Without it she was certain this beautiful, healthy baby would never have been born.

Seventeen years of answering questions and listening to accusations of barrenness from family and associates, seventeen years of trying, and failing, to conceive a child had led her to Master Visser, and after 15 days of torturing her taste buds a miracle had happened.

Now looking down at her new born son she remembered how she had gagged while trying to swallow the disgusting mixture and how relieved she had been when the paper cone was empty.

Those who had scorned her for her barreness, marvelled at the baby.

'After all this time,' they muttered. 'So beautiful, and all those blond curls. He'll grow into a handsome young man, just like his father.'

Even her husband was surprised.

But she told no one her secret.

* * * * *

Jill laughed when the mirror glazed over.

'I think the effect of that mixture must have carried over to this life time,' she said'

'Can you imagine how I felt when the sonographer doing my scan pointed out two babies in my womb and then announced that she thought there were more? My husband Jim let go of my hand and asked, 'How many more?'

'Well I can clearly see three and I think I am picking up four heart beats, 'she said, 'so I'm just going to get my colleague to come and assist me.'

'When she left the room we sat in shocked silence and then I remember saying, 'I'll need to turn into an octopus to hold all their hands when I take them shopping.'

'For some reason, nerves I suppose, we found this idea hilarious and we were laughing uncontrollably when the staff returned.'

'What if there are five?" said Jim and that set us off laughing again.'

'There were four, and now three years later there is another on the way' she said patting her bump.

'I'm not exactly barren this time round am I?' she laughed.

I knew Marcus Belldon, he was a solicitor and a family friend. In fact he and my father played golf together most weekends. He was a friendly man but had never shown any interest in my business so I was surprised when he telephoned and said he would like to book a sitting.

When he arrived he asked if he could tell me something before the session began and of course I agreed.

'I have always loved the sea,' he said. 'I was brought up in a small town in Cornwall and although I always wanted to be a solicitor I also wanted to join the life boat crew. My mother was not at all pleased about this, not even when I said I would learn the ropes but just be part of the relief team ready to go in case someone was ill or away on holiday when a flare went up.'

'That's just what your father said, and your brother too,' she replied and look what happened to him.'

'I pointed out to her as gently as I could that Phil had been killed in a car crash on his way to the life boat station and had not lost his life at sea. And before you say anything,' I added,' I know if he hadn't joined the relief crew he wouldn't have been on Haydn Way going to that training session when that lorry went out of control. But he might have stopped off at the Haydn Arms for a pint on the way home from work and still have been involved in that pile up.'

'As for Dad,' I said to her, 'he survived twenty years as coxswain and never once fell in the sea.'

My mother shook her head. 'It's the worry,' she said. 'When I hear that siren I worry for those in trouble at sea and for the safety of the crew who are going to help them.'

'When your Dad retired I had only those at sea to pray for. Please don't put me through that again.'

I didn't join the crew, something I suppose I have always regretted.

I had a small sailing boat before the children were born and we have been on several cruises but there is something about being near the sea and even more especially actually on the sea that makes me wonder if I had been a sailor in a past life.'

We sat facing the mirror and I truly expected to see waves and maybe even a ship so I was surprised when an image of a junk shop appeared. The window was full of a variety of objects and there were more piled up on the pavement outside.

* * * * *

THE JUNK SHOP

A man, who looked liked like Marcus was studying the items on the pavement and then he entered the shop and wandered around occasionally stopping to look at something and then moving on again. From behind an old sofa he pulled out a long wooden box.

He turned to the aging proprietor and asked what was in it.

The man shrugged, 'Can't remember,' he said, 'Been there for ages.'

'Mind if I have a look inside?' asked Marcus.

The old man nodded and hobbled across to the box. He brushed away the dust with his handkerchief and slowly returned to his chair.

Marcus was busy examining the outside of the box.
'This looks familiar to me,' he said to himself, and then gasped as he lifted the lid.

Inside was a polished brass telescope, shiny and dust free.

Marcus turned to the old man. 'Unless I am very much mistaken I know what this is,' he said. 'I am sure that on the underside of this treasure the initials PRD are engraved. I know this because it was mine. I used it when I was the captain of a sailing ship called 'The Falcon' in the nineteenth century.

Marcus lifted the telescope from its box and carried it to where the man was sitting. He turned it over and revealed the letters PRD.

* * * **

Marcus sat beside me shaking his head and with tears running down his face.

135

'That was amazing,' he said. 'It answered my question as to why I was so interested in being at sea and has also given me information that could lead to me finding out exactly who I was in that past life.'

He paid me and gave me a huge tip too!

I shall call my next client simply Lady B. She is in fact a Lady, married to a very wealthy Lord. She grew up in a large house surrounded by an extensive garden to play in and with servants at her beck and call. Money had never been a problem when she was young and certainly wasn't now but she confessed that she was, and always had been, afraid of becoming poor. She was hoping a past life regression could explain this fear to her.

* * * * *

They called it The Pavilion, though in actual fact it was little more than a very large garden shed to which they had added embellishments.

Some of their friends called them pretentious but those friends never refused an invitation for drinks and nibbles in the pavilion. They knew wine and beer would flow freely and the food was always delicious.

The midsummer party, as always had been a great success.

Nobody mentioned the absence of the Whitely catering team who were usually hovering about, eager to top up glasses and pass round platters of food. That was something to be discussed at a later date.

Today was the day to congratulate Madge on the excellent spread of food she had prepared.

Several of the guests noticed the wine was served in decanters rather than, as in previous years, bottles displaying the age and origin of the liquor within. Something else to ponder about on another occasion.

As the last of their guests hugged them goodbye Madge and Gerry both sighed and then they started the task of clearing the debris.

Gone were the days when caterers provided the food and returned to collect the dirty dishes and glasses.

Tonight had been hard, and both of them felt they deserved an Oscar for the way they had happily joined in the banter and merriment while passing around the food and pouring the drinks.

They had used up some of their precious savings to pay for the party, the last one they would ever hold in The Pavilion.

With bankruptcy looming closer every time they received a bill, they ate mince instead of rump steak and drank tea in the evenings instead of champagne.

The money Gerry had made during Prohibition was dwindling away and they would no longer be able to keep up the appearance of being an affluent couple.

They both knew that once word got round that they were selling their house those 'friends' who had enjoyed the midsummer parties in The Pavilion would quickly erase them from their invitation list for social events and they would become outcasts.

* * * * *

Lady B smiled. 'It seems in the past I lived a life of luxury in The States, existing on ill gotten gains, gains that were eventually lost and most likely catapulted me into poverty.'

'I do hope I was Gerry and not Madge, can't abide that name. Awful friend of my mother insisted I called her Aunty Madge when I was young. Never liked the name since then.'

'I'd certainly rather have been Gerry, making my fortune as a bootlegger. I

138

might come back another day and see if you can discover if I ran a speakeasy in the 1920's. Who knows I may have met Al Capone.'

'That's something to tell my therapist at my next appointment and something for her to work on with me.'

Lady B picked up her fur coat, extracted a cheque, made out to me, from her expensive looking handbag and signalled to her security guard who had been standing outside my unit that she was ready to leave.

THE CURIOUS MAN-
Stan said, 'I'm fascinated by the prospect of past lives and looking forward to what you are going to tell me.'

* * * * *

THE STATUE
It was bathed in moonlight as the lovers, arms entwined, sauntered across the deserted market square towards the statue. In the morning people would be hurrying to work, others would be setting up their stalls to sell fruit, vegetables, flowers and other goods. None of them would have time to glance at the majestic figure, high above them on its marble plinth.

139

This stature had been unveiled more than a century ago with great pomp and ceremony. It was fashioned in bronze by a then virtually unknown artist, Christopher Dulon, and it was said to have extraordinary powers.

Christopher's name is now, of course, recognised around the globe but the mysterious benefactor who commissioned this piece of work has never been revealed.

He is known as Mr X, and he provided the money for the stature and the secret location where the figure was made.

Christopher designed the stature and while it was under construction Mr X made provisions for annual scholarships to be awarded to four local pupils so they could carry on their education after the age of 14 at the local grammar school. This money would be there, in perpetuity, as long as his name was never revealed to the public.

In return the town of Stalridge agreed to allow a massive plinth to be erected in the market place and for Dolan's work to be seated upon it.

Joseph Parker was an enigma and his descendants often wondered if he had been the anonymous benefactor. They had written evidence that he was one of the meanest mill owners in the county. There were begging letters from sacked employees, newspaper reports detailing court cases where he had triumphed over tenants in his properties, and photographs showing him scowling at the camera.

But along side all those negative references to him they had paperwork which provided evidence that he had a benevolent side to him as well. Money was given to a local orphanage. There were bequests in his will for workers who had served him loyally throughout their years of employment in his mill and more importantly a vague reference to some sort of scholarships he had set up.

Mr X eventually married late in life. Legend has it that when younger he had been unlucky in love, left waiting at the altar on his wedding day for his fiancé who changed her mind about marrying him at the very last minute.

Mr X did not want others to suffer as he had. So when the Stalridge statue was being made, it was imbibed with the power to open hearts and enrich them with feelings of everlasting love.

Those hurrying past it to work each day have no time for such sentiment but lovers often approach it by the light of the moon to receive its blessing.

* * * * *

Stan was smiling. So I may have been an artist, a jilted benefactor or a lover who visited the statute. Perhaps one day I'll find out which one I was.

THE NEW AGE SCEPTIC
Sarah was another client who wanted to see into her near future.

'I think all this crystal healing and incense burning is a lot of new age nonsense but I have no idea what to do with my life and my partner who believes in all that weird stuff you do has insisted that I come to see you but quite honestly I think it is a waste of your time, my time and his money,' she said when she arrived.

Her attitude was so negative and the energy surrounding her so heavy I was not sure the mirror would be able to help but to my surprise the following scenario unfolded.

....

THE INHERITANCE
Sarah was standing outside a building with a large banner attached to the

railings, which said, 'Mind, Body and Spirit Fair' here today.'

Somewhat reluctantly she entered and looked around the crowded room. There were stalls selling crystals, jewellery, drums and various people waving their hands over prostrate bodies, seemingly healing them.

There were also several banners behind the tables where mediums were giving readings. She wondered how on earth she could choose the right person to help her.

She looked round again and one lady caught her eye. She had a small fluffy dog sitting on her lap and both she and the dog were wearing bright pink outfits and had a silver bow on top of their heads.

She approached the pair, still not sure if this was a good idea.

She sat down, smiled at the dog before making eye contact with 'Roxanne, International Medium, TV sensation and mentor to the stars.'

'I'd just like a mini reading,' she said.

Roxanne passed Sarah a pack of cards.

'Please shuffle them, think about your question or problem while you do so and then when you are ready choose just one card from the pack.'

Sarah mixed up the cards, all the time thinking, "What shall I do? What shall I do?'

Then she drew a card from the middle of the pack and handed it to the medium.

Roxanne turned it over and the word FASHION was written above a picture of a woman dressed in what was obviously expensive clothing.

Roxanne began to talk.

'I have a woman with me who had a lifelong love of clothes, shoes and accessories. She loved to look elegant wherever she went.'

'She is showing me a picture of herself wearing a mini skirt, a very mini, mini skirt. She says she spent all her money on being fashionable and she enjoyed being looked at, admired and talked about. She is holding several coat hangers with dresses and trousers hanging off them and at her feet there are many pairs of shoes and handbags.'

'She says she is sorry she spent all her money but asks that you enjoy your inheritance.'

Roxanne smiled and started to pat her dog.

Sarah realised her reading was over and handed the medium a ten pound note, all the while visualising the six wardrobes she had found when she had gone into Aunt Jo's house. Each wardrobe was overflowing with items that would once have been the highly fashionable. There were dozens of shoes lined up in pairs, dresses, flared trousers, kaftans, and an array of coats and jackets.

In a daze she left the mind, body and spirit show.

* * * * *

Sarah sat shaking her head. I wasn't sure if that was a negative reaction or one of shock.

Finally she spoke.

'That was surreal. My father's sister, Jo, recently died .We knew very little about her as she had been a bit of a rebel in the 1960s and the family severed all ties with her after she was involved in some scandal. Surprisingly she has left me all her belongings, even though she never met me'

'Her house was rented and needs to be cleared as soon as possible so I went to look to see what needs to be removed and there really are five or six wardrobes containing many pieces of clothing and other fashion items.'

She sat in silence, shaking her head again and then said, 'I'm guessing all that stuff is what you would call vintage or something like that and is probably worth quite a bit of money. I think I could use it to stock a shop.'

Several weeks after her session Sarah came to see me. She had some business cards for her shop, 'Dedicated Follower Of fashion', and asked if I would put some on display. In return she took some of my promo and promised to hand it to her customers.

THE ANGRY MAN
Martin said, "I had this thing done once before and it was a load of old rubbish and it cost me a fortune. That crazy female said I was a woman in a previous life but I know for a fact I have never been in a woman's body. Look at me I am ALL man. It was a load of old clap trap and I couldn't get my money back cos there was no way to prove what that woman told me was wrong. '

'So I have come to you so you can show me that if I have lived before it was not as a woman. I've brought my sister

146

with me so she can see for herself I was not a woman.'

I tried to explain to this angry client that he had maybe lived many times and it was highly likely that at least one of them had been as a woman.

'I cannot promise that you will see a life today where you are a man. So do you still wish to go ahead with the session?' I asked.

He nodded and we began.
* * * * *

THE FISHWIFE
The image in the mirror was dark. It showed a row of women, wearing tartan headscarves , all busy gutting fish. They threw the waste into a nearby container and placed the filleted fish in a barrel filled with salt. Their hands were red raw and as they worked, they were constantly complaining about their low wages.
* * * * *

'There you are again as a woman dealing with fish,' the sister said. 'So what you saw before is the truth."

As soon as she spoke the image in the mirror vanished.

She carried on, 'I always thought your macho behaviour covered up some secret from your past, and that life we

147

have just seen probably explains why you won't eat fish. It is just your pride that's hurting, knowing that you were once a woman,' and she laughed at him.

Martin stood up, flexed his muscles, lifted his tee shirt to reveal a bronzed hairy chest and said "I tell you I am ALL man,' then without another word he walked out.

His sister looked at me. 'That was exactly what he saw last time and so it must be true,' she laughed again. "He'll never live this down. Macho Martin was a fishwife."

Needless to say I never saw Martin or his sister again, and they left without paying me paid me!

THE WRITER WITH WRITER'S BLOCK

Clancey Mason came to me on the recommendation of Fiona Strange.

'She said your therapy helped her overcome writers block and that's just what I'm suffering from at the moment. Ten novels under my belt, all best sellers and I haven't got a clue what number eleven will be about, not the vaguest idea,' he sighed. 'So please can you work your magic and enlighten me as to my future?"

'I can't promise anything but we can start of by looking in my mirror and see if any images appear.' I told him.

* * * * *

THE FAKE MEDICINE MEN

They drove their wagon into town and pulled up in front of the chapel. A young man with a mop of ginger hair jumped down from the cart, pulled off a table and set it down by the chapel gate, as quietly as he could so as not to disturb those who were singing inside the nearby building.

His companion, an older rather plump gentleman, tied the horse to some railings and then unloaded an assortment of boxes and bottles onto the table.

Their timing was perfect. When the doors opened to release the congregation the newcomers were standing behind their laden table.

Tied to the railings next to the horse was a large banner that read," Doctor Murphy's Miracle medicines. Our pills and potions cure everything.'

Myra Higgs nodded to her friend, Josie Jane, 'Quack doctors,' she said. 'I've seen it all before. They sell us fake medicine and then gallop away, leaving us as sick and as sore as before but poorer by many dollars.'

Josie Jane, ignored Myra and went to join the crowd milling around the table, listening to Doctor Murphy's patter, picking up bottles, smelling their content and parting with their hard earned money.

'Incredible,' said Myra to herself. 'They come to me for my herbs and concoctions, because others say I have cured them but they never have a spare cent to pay me for my services. Yet when the fake medicine men arrive in town these same people have money in their purses!'

She turned away from the scene which faded before our eyes.

* * * * *

'Interesting,' said Clancey, 'that was supposed to be a future life progression and yet what we saw was obviously in the States and certainly at least a century ago from now. I'm thinking there is perhaps the making of a story there which, in the future, maybe even tonight, I might start to write.

What was interesting to me was that Doctor Murphy was the splitting image of Clancey, something he hadn't noticed. He thought he had just been given an

150

idea for a story, which he would write in the future but my feeling was that in some way he had, in a previous life, been part of the scenario we had just witnessed.

This was something I had never encountered before, a future life progression showing a past life regression to aid someone in their future! Bizarre!

Two weeks later I received a text which simply said. "12,000 words written of my novel entitled, "'The Trial of The Fake Medicine Men.

' Thank you and thank you Clancey. Oh and by the way my friend Bridget will be coming to see you.

'Soon you will be able to advertise that you are- by appointment to people suffering with a writer's block-' and he finished his message with several smiley faced emojis.

THE ALIEN

Barney was convinced he was an alien and to be honest his features were slightly unusual, as was his manner of speaking. Sometimes, when he was feeling stressed, he ran all his words together so a sentence sounded like one long word, at other times he spoke with a very jerky voice.

People who knew him had, over the years, got used to him and realised they wouldn't understand everything he said.

He was interested in being regressed to see if he had in fact been an alien in another life and maybe still had some of that creature's DNA in his present body.

I explained about my mirror and he was willing to see what happened. What we saw was amazing.

* * * * *

THE ZIGNELIAN

The soil was blue, the vegetation yellow and there were large insect like creatures moving across the landscape.

Although their bodies were blue so they merged in with the soil, their many red legs and the single vivid green eye made them quite conspicuous. They looked like something a young child with a new set of felt tip pens would draw.

These creatures seemed to be converging on a strange purple object. Suddenly there were voices, high pitched and very jerky.

'HurryhurryforwemustnotbelateHurryh ewillbeleavingsoon.'

Almost at once the meaning of these strange sounds became clear. It was as though they were being translated into English for us to understand.

'Hurry, hurry, we must not be late. Hurry he will be leaving soon'

* * * * *

The mirror clouded over and when the mist cleared we saw an image of a very young looking boy. He was, I'd estimate 5 or 6 years old and was sitting in a bedroom reading a book.

The temperature in Talking Rainbows suddenly dropped several degrees and I found myself shivering. Barney looked at the mirror as a strange voice began to speak.

* * * * *

'In exactly 12 days you will be contacted by a being from Planet Zignel. It has already set off on its long journey from our planet to yours. We have tried our best to transmute it so it resembles a human, so it can mingle with the beings on earth, but as it approaches you the energy around you will change and you will be able to see the true appearance of it.

DO NOT BE AFRAID!

The being comes in peace. You have been chosen from billions of bodies on earth to be contacted by us. We have given the being your name, Barney, because it will walk up to you and walk into your body to become a part of the human Barney.

We wish to work with you, share our philosophies of life, and our healing tools. We have the ability to manipulate energy in a way planet earth has never seen before.

Once you, the human Barney have merged with the Zignelian Barney you will work together and you may notice certain changes, maybe in the way you speak, the way you think and certainly in what you are able to do.

We wish you both every success in this experiment.'

* * * * *

Barney had a huge smile on his face.

'It looks like it's not just a remnant of DNA from a past life that is in my body but I am in fact maybe as much as half, or even more, an alien,' he said in his jerky voice.

'That explains a lot,' he said while nodding his head.

'I have always felt different to other people, even when I was a child. My mother had me tested, anxious to get a label put on me but there wasn't one that suited. I guess they don't have one for alien." He smiled again.

'I once heard her tell a neighbour that it was as though I had come from another planet!'

''But when I say I heard my Mum'' I wasn't eaves dropping behind the door, no this is just something that happens to me from time to time. I can tune into what people are saying even if I am a long way away from them. I just hear their words or their thoughts inside my head.'

'That's how I knew about the trick my sister was planning to play on me and it was the first time I used one of my other secret powers.'

'I was sitting on my bed stoking the cat one afternoon when inside my head I heard Kelly talking to her mate Lucy on her the phone.

'Barney's a bit of a wimp she said. 'So I've made a terrifying monster- I used quick drying clay and it's bright blue. I've given it huge fangs and big red eyes. I'm going to put it under his bed. When he finds it he'll go crazy with fear.'

Then they both began to laugh.

'And,' continued Kelly, 'just before he goes to sleep, I'm going to stand outside his door and growl like a dinosaur. He'll be so scared he'll wet himself when he hears that.'

They both began to giggle again.

But I was chuckling too because they didn't know what I knew and they didn't know what the voice inside my head had made me practice over and over again. They just didn't realise what I could do when I put my right middle finger in my ear!

Before getting in bed that night I peered under my bed. Sure enough Kelly's creation was there.

As I always slept with my door slightly open I heard when Kelly open her door and started to creep along the landing towards my room.

I quickly put my finger in my ear.
There was the sound of something
moving under my bed. I bent down and
pointed with my left hand towards my
door. The monster appeared from under
the bed and obediently started walking
towards the door. I could hear Kelly
breathing outside my door, obviously
getting ready to make her scary monster
noises.

The creature got as far as the door
and edged its way through the crack,
and that is when my sister screamed.

I left my finger in my ear until I heard
Mum come rushing up the stairs and
then I removed it, lay down and
pretended to be asleep.

Kelly was gabbling about the monster
moving and trying to get her, the big
baby, and Mum was making soothing
noises about nightmares and sleep
walking.

'But it was under his bed,' my sister
kept repeating.
'Well obviously Barney found it and put
it outside his room, said Mum.

Actually I've always thought my Mum should have been cross with Kelly for trying to scare ME, instead of comforting her.

Mum took Kelly back to her room and after a few minutes I sensed her looking through the crack in my door to make sure I was asleep. Then she went down stairs and I heard her tell my father what all the commotion had been about.

I put my finger into my ear again and beckoned with my left hand. The monster trotted obediently back under my bed.

'What monster?' I asked, feigning innocence, when they discovered the creature was under my bed the next morning.

And that is just one of the times I have used that power.

I'll let you into a secret, some nights I go to parks or along the streets and using what I call 'my finger in the ear technique' I move all the rubbish into a single pile so it can easily be cleared in the morning. There are other things I can do because of what I now know is the other Barney inside me but they have to remain a secret.

'Could you show me?' I begged him.

'Slip off your shoes and leave them by the chair,' he ordered and when I had done that he told me to go and stand by the entrance.

Once I was there he put his finger into his right ear and then pointed at my shoes. To my surprise (yes I must admit it all sounded rather far fetched) my shoes slowly moved across the floor towards my feet. Once they had arrived Barney removed the finger from his ear and the shoes immediately stopped moving.

I thought my mirror was a miracle but this totally astounded me.

'There are enormous potentials for this technique, especially for the clearing of litter and plastic contamination in the sea and rivers," said Barney but before today I was too nervous of being ridiculed to tell anyone.

However now I know there are others with Zignelians implanted in them I think somehow I need to contact them and maybe if we use our powers we can change the world.

I asked Barney to keep in touch but to date I have heard nothing more from him.

* * * * *

<u>THE DIARY</u>

Sybil's diary 4th March 1900- I am VERY cross with Elsie May. I thought we were best friends. I walk to school with her, sit next to her and help her tie her boot laces when they come undone.

Sometimes when Mam doesn't have enough money for bread and I only have a hard boiled egg for my lunch Elsie May will give me one of her sandwiches.

That's what best friends do.

Today I had a big secret inside me and I told it to my best friend. I know what I said was true and when I'd whispered it to her, I told her it was a secret and she must never tell anyone else.

But while we were in the yard at playtime she shouted out my secret so everyone could hear, even the boys in their side of the playground. I know they all heard because John Michael whispered a bad word at me when I walked past him in class.

I will get my revenge on Elsie May. I don't know how at the moment but some day I will humiliate her and make her feel as bad as I did today.

Sybil's diary 6th June 1929- I should, I am sure, feel ashamed of myself. My behaviour today could be considered despicable but then Elsie May's attitude to me, Lady Harcourt, was really inappropriate.

I know we were at school together, best friends for a short while, but I haven't seen her for probably ten or twelve years.

She is Elsie May Rushton, a spinster and a shop assistant and I am Sybil, Lady Harcroft from the manor house.

The familiarity she showed me today was unacceptable and I felt duty bound to complain to her superior in case she behaves in a similar manner to someone else above her status.

The manager of the shop defended Elsie May saying she was obviously so excited to see an old friend after all these years and that is why she greeted me so exuberantly.

However, I insisted she be sacked. I intend to spend a lot of money in the furnishing department now we are renovating the manor and I can't be embarrassed like that every time I go into the shop, nor do I wish to be constantly reminded of the day Elsie May shouted out my secret.

At last I have my revenge.

* * * * *

Poor Grace looked shocked when the mirror clouded over.

'Interesting story but quite frankly I don't like to think I was either of those two women. Is there any way I can be regressed to another time where only one of them is present so I can see which of the two was me?'

'Let me try,' I said.

'If I regress you using the traditional method and get you back to say 1940 we might strike lucky and find out who you were.

Grace walked over the Bridge of Time and stepped off in 1940. This is the story that unfolded using my questions and her answers.

* * * * *

'Where are you?'

'I am standing in front of my house and a boy is riding up the drive on his bike. Oh no it's a telegraph boy'

'What has he brought for you?'

162

'It's a telegram and I'm frightened to open it?'

'Do you want to stay and see what it says or go back to the bridge?'

'I will open it."

'What does it say?'

'Oh! It's wonderful news, my son has two days leave and is already on a train. He says he will be at the Manor by dinner time tonight.'

* * * * *

I brought Grace back over the bridge to the present day.

'Well it looks as though I had rather a nasty streak in me when I was last here on earth;'.

'I'd love to know what my secret was that Elsie May shouted out in the playground,' she said. 'It must have been very important for me to harbour a grudge against her for all those years.'

'I guess I must have reincarnated quite quickly after that life. I hope Elsie May didn't too, or if she did not round here because I don't want to run into her again.'

True to his word Clancey sent his friend Brenda for a session. She too was spending hours each day waiting for

inspiration to strike so she could begin
her next novel.

'It's never happened to me before,' she
confessed.

'Usually the words I want to write are
in my head before I sit down at my desk,
but recently all I do is sit and doodle and
that really stressed me.'

'Let's see if the mirror can help in any
way.' I said.

* * * * *

This time the latch moved on the door.
So many times he had touched it,
pushed it and rattled it but all in vain.
He had not been able to lift the latch,
open the door and escape from this hell
hole.

Why he had kept trying he didn't
know, but it seemed as though at last his
perseverance had paid off.

At some time during the night one of
the conquistador rebels had crept up to
the door and shot open the bolt on the
other side that had been keeping it shut.

Now he had to consider carefully the
implication of this, before making a bid
for freedom.

Was this a trap?

Were the enemy testing him, lying in
wait and hoping he would escape so they

would be justified in killing him as an escaping prisoner?

He didn't know where his companions were. Maybe they were also prisoners.

Maybe they were all dead.

He had no idea where he was as he'd been blindfolded throughout the long journey here. He wondered what the terrain was like outside and which way he should run if he decided to risk leaving the prison.

He wanted freedom, but he wanted to live and so he decided to wait a few more hours, listening carefully for any noises outside.

* * * * *

The scene faded and I said, 'Oh no, I wanted to know more, did he go or did he stay in that prison?'

Brenda was smiling. 'Now I remember it all,' she said.

'The incident that led up to me being put in that prison and everything that happened after I discovered the door was no longer bolted.'

'Did you leave?" I asked.

Brenda smiled. 'You'll have to wait until I have written the novel and then I'll send you a free hard back copy. In fact I'll dedicate the book to you!'

165

THE BROTHER

My brother, Giles, ever the sceptic and always eager to mock me, for my 'new age ideas', came to visit one lunch time. As we sat talking the mirror clouded over and we saw a scarecrow standing in a field. It began to talk to us.

* * * * *

THE SCARECROW

I am all alone in this field. It is a lonely existence and rather an uncomfortable one too. My arms are stretched out day and night. My body is made of itchy straw and I am sure I've some squatters living in my left leg. I've felt them scampering around and squeaking as they did so.

The smile is set on my face so I can't show my disapproval by frowning and my eyes always look straight ahead so I can't see the invaders.

For the first few days after I was planted, here, and I use the word deliberately as a hole was dug, I was put in and then the earth was packed firmly around me so I will stay firm and upright, the wind was really strong and my hat nearly blew off.

Fortunately the considerate person who made me had tied it firmly to my

166

smiling head so although it moved about it didn't fly away.

Do I do a good job standing here in this field? I have no idea as no seeds have yet been planted around me. To be honest I am looking forward to the day when they are sown as then, hopefully birds will come to visit me and I won't be so lonely.

* * * * *

The vision faded and Giles and I looked at each other.

'What on earth was that all about?' I asked.

Giles looked behind him.

'Did you project that from somewhere onto the mirror?' he asked.

'Certainly not,' I replied. 'I told you this is what has been happening ever since I opened Talking Rainbows. The mirror that Dad fixed to that far wall has been showing people their past and future lives.'

'But, 'I emphasised, 'the tales told have always been about people. Never before has the mirror shown an inanimate object.'

My brother shrugged. 'Always said you were weird Sis and this just proves it. Are you and your mirror implying I

167

was a scarecrow in a previous life or will be one in future?' he laughed.

I shook my head. No in your case I think this was a symbolic message. You spend a lot of time on your own. You are not happy where you live because of the noisy neighbours in the flat below. That could be the significance of the mice in the scarecrow's legs.

You say you can't move because you work from home and a hundred and one other reasons. You are stuck in a job that makes you tired, just as the scarecrow is unable to move out of the field.

It's all there in what we have just seen and my dear Giles there is an obvious message for you. Plant some seeds, by that I mean start applying for other jobs and things will change'

(I must confess I was rather pleased with my analysis of that strange scenario and Giles was looking thoughtful.)

'Maybe you and your mirror are not so batty after all, 'he said.

'Everything you said is true and believe it or not just recently I have seen four different adverts for graphic designer jobs that would involve working in an office instead of at home, but of course I didn't even consider applying for them.'

'Thanks Sis, you have given me food for thought.

Seems I might have converted my brother to my New Age way of life!

(Update- Giles applied for all four jobs, got interviews at three of them and was offered a job by two companies.)

He is now working in an office, has moved into a semi detached house, is in charge of an advertising campaign and is smiling all the time as he is happier than I have seen him for many years.)

That session with Giles was the first of several that involved objects rather than people. I was able to help the police solve a crime from a vision I saw, one lunch time, about the death of a young boy.

* * * * *

THE SHOPPING TROLLEY

I believe tonight is the night I'll be featured on Crimewatch. Well of course another trolley has been used for reconstructing the crime, I'm in no fit state to do that job. But just before the programme ends there will be some shots of me, taken right there where they found me, on my side and missing a wheel..

169

A smart blond reporter has been covering the case along side several policemen, some in white coats and one who seems to think I am unimportant, but let's face it without me there would be no crime to investigate.

That Wednesday was quite a normal day. It started at midnight because we are a 24/7 supermarket. It was icy in the car park and on nights like that I always appreciate being taken into the warmth of the shop. I had a few loads, nothing too heavy.

Day time, as usual, was busy and several times I was full to overflowing. I transported one annoying toddler who wouldn't sit still in my seat and another who kept kicking me. I locked my wheels to show my displeasure but when his mother started kicking me as well. I quickly unlocked them again so she could get her shopping done as quickly as possible and unload her brat along with her shopping.

So really just an ordinary day until about 4p.m. when there was the usual post school pick up rush.

Three hooded youths came into the car park, their arms were linked and they slouched over to the trolley shelter. I was next in line and sensed trouble

They kept their heads turned away from the CTV cameras as they began to push me away from the shop entrance. They wheeled me out of the car park and as soon as they were out of sight one of the boys said, 'Get in the cart.'

'I don't want to,' said another voice. 'Do what I say Fatty Phil, get in or you will be really sorry,' shouted the first boy.

Someone began to cry.

'Grab his other arm Mark, let's stuff him in this trolley and give him the ride of his life.'

I felt the weight of his body as it was thrown into me and then the other two boys began to run really fast, pushing me and my cargo ahead of them.

I bumped over the tarmac and tried to lock my wheels but they were turning far too fast.

I was out of control.

The boys were laughing and swearing as they ran and I heard one of them, I think it was the boy Mark, as it wasn't a voice I had heard before, suggest they go down to the canal tow path.

They swung me round and began to run even faster than before. The path was uneven, potholes and stones everywhere. Suddenly I bumped into something hard, I suspect it was a rock and I felt my front wheel sheer off.

I tried to stay upright, really I did, but I couldn't stop and I fell heavily onto my side. The full weight of the boy crashed into my metal framework and then he rolled out.

I heard a splash.

A voice from the water called. 'Help, Jeff, Mark, help me please.'

But the only response to that was the sound of feet running away.

The voice called out again and again and then there was silence.

I lay there all night. The moon shone down and early in the morning icy crystals formed on my metal frame. Just

after dawn I felt some of the frost melt
as a dog lifted its leg against me.

Then I heard a voice say, 'Oh no,' and
shortly after there was chaos all around
me. Footsteps, more voices, crying, and
flashes from cameras. I feared the worst.

Of course it's not the crime of stealing
me that will be featured tonight, but I
am part of the tale and if you watch
you'll see my ten seconds of fame, right
there on your TV.

* * * * *

I wasn't sure whether to phone the
police. I was worried they might be like
my brother and think I was a New Age
freak.

I decided to wait and watch the
programme that evening. The shopping
trolley incident was the first crime
shown and I knew then that I had to
phone the number given out at the end.

I was interviewed and although I'm
sure the detective thought I was wasting
his time, my statement did lead them to
two boys from Phil's class named Jeff
and Mark and they admitted they had

bullied him and run away from the canal after the trolley had tipped over.

There was a report in the local paper about the trial of the two boys for manslaughter. It mentioned that a local therapist helped the police solve The Shopping Trolley crime. Word got out that the therapist was me and now I have to keep my phone permanently on silence when I am at work as so many people want to book a session with me.

THE FATHER

Peter Cooper enquired whether a future life progression session could show him a possible future for his daughter and granddaughter.

'I worry about their future now I'm getting older and it would give me peace of mind if I knew that my somewhat wayward, unhappy daughter and my wonderful grandchild were going to be happy,' he confessed.

'We can try,' I said, thinking the mirror might oblige as it seemed capable of almost anything we asked of it.

* * * * *

THE EXPLORER

Peter Cooper smiled to himself. He knew the rule, no favourites were allowed but of all his six grandchildren this little girl at his side, so intent on learning about the world she inhabited, had a special place in his heart.

He glanced at his watch. Frankie, his daughter was due to arrive any minute to collect them but they were last in the slow moving queue of people waiting to have their booked signed.

He wished there was a chair nearby so he could sit down but this was Gloria's birthday treat, and if she wanted a signed book, then he was prepared to stand in this queue to ensure she got one.

It had been a strange request from the six year old, but ever since she had heard that Explorer Jo was coming to the local library she had been begging to go and see him.

The adult audience had been enthralled during his talk and Gloria had listened with a wise look on her face, as if the speaker was confirming everything she knew.

Her favourite TV programmes were the ones about wild life and other countries and Explorer Jo featured in many of the ones she had enjoyed since she and her mother had moved in with her grandfather.

Peter looked at his watch again. His daughter had pleaded with him to take Gloria to the library saying she had no interest in Explorer Jo.

'I can't sit for an hour listening to someone make out he is a hero just because he climbed a famous mountain in his pyjamas and slippers,' she explained.

Gloria had laughed, 'That's not what he did,' she giggled.

The queue inched forward and. Peter glanced towards the door. Typical of his daughter to be late.

Explorer Joe made a point of talking to everyone when signing their book. His arm was aching and he was thirsty.

He glanced up and saw an elderly gentleman talking earnestly to a child.

He had noticed her during his talk. Normally his daytime audiences were composed of middle aged women, so this little girl with her red hair and solemn expression had really intrigued him

'I'll give her one of my DVDs as well as signing her book,' he thought.

Frankie paused outside the library.

Where were her father and Gloria?

The talk should have finished some time ago and she only had 15 minutes left on the parking meter. She realised she would have to go in and get them and that was truly the last thing she wanted to do.

'Explorer Jo! Trust Jack Wallis to change his name to something more exotic,' she thought.

He had been plain old Jack at Uni, part of her gang, always a dare devil, always game to go one step further than anyone else but careful to never break the law.

During their last two terms in Southampton they had been an item, and he had been a kind, loving and generous boyfriend.

He had tried to tame his wildness during their relationship, restricting his excursions to occasional weekend trips with his mates, fully understanding that Frankie had a thirst for knowledge not thrills.

While others were envying her for being in a relationship with Jack she was daydreaming about their possible future together.

Those dreams disappeared the day Jack saw an advert in the newspaper. A TV company were looking for a male and a female student to represent the 20 plus age group in a reality programme.

Five men and five women, born a decade apart, were to explore a remote area of South America. They were to exchange ideas and skills to see how the different age groups interacted in unfamiliar circumstances.

Jack pleaded with Frankie to apply with him but she knew it wasn't for her. She in turn begged him not to enter, fearing that if he was selected she would lose him.

He applied, was chosen and their proposed gap year trip was abandoned.

Frankie found a holiday job at a local chemists and used her staff discount to buy a pregnancy test.

Jack went exploring and became famous.

By the time Gloria was born Jack was the new face in reality TV, His letters stopped coming as the offers of work poured in and when he chose to change his name to Explorer Jo, Frankie took on the title of 'single mum'.

She pulled her hat over her forehead, took a deep breath and entered the library. She could see her father near the signing table and Explorer Jo bent over a book. Her heart leapt as memories flooded back.

'Shall I go and tell them to hurry up, or leave now and move the car? The one thing I can't do is go and join them?'

Peter turned and noticing his daughter waved to her and pointed to a nearby chair. Frankie didn't move. Peter beckoned to her and with a sigh of relief went to sit in the chair leaving Gloria alone in the queue.

Frankie hesitated and then went to stand beside her daughter who had just reached the book signing table.

Jo glanced up. It was that young girl he had noticed in the audience but she was no longer accompanied by the elderly man. A woman with a hat pulled really low over her eyes was holding the child's hand.

He smiled .

'What name would you, like me to write in the book?' he asked.

'I'm Gloria," she said, 'but please write my mummy's name, Frankie Cooper, because she had to work today and she missed your talk.'

His pen stopped mid stroke and his heart felt as if it was stopping too.

During the past few years of adventure and fame he had never forgotten his first love, never if truth be told stopped loving her.

He tilted his head so he could see under the woman's ridiculous hat and smiling he rushed round the table to hug her tightly.

His eyes then returned to the red haired little girl standing open mouthed beside them. He looked puzzled, as he flicked a lock of his own red hair from his eyes and he turned to look at Frankie. She gave a slight nod, I didn't tell you because you were busy exploring the world and being famous.' She whispered

He looked back at Gloria and said, 'Now I have finished signing books I am going to the café because I am very thirsty. Would you and your Mummy like to come with me?'

'Can we Mummy, can we?'Gloria demanded.

Frankie took a deep breath, smiled at her long lost friend and said, 'I don't see why not. Go and wait with Grandpa and I will join you in a minute.'

'Please, let her just enjoy being with you, her hero, today. We can talk about what we obviously need to talk about at a later date when she isn't with us.'

Explorer Jo had a huge grin on his face as he nodded in agreement.
* * * * *

Peter had tears in his eyes as the scene faded from the mirror.

'It seems as though it's going to turn out to be alright,' he said.

'I had no idea who Gloria's father was, no idea at all, Frankie never ever told me. I just knew he broke her heart.'

'I've seen that chap on various TV programmes. Now I don't know whether to drop some hints to Frankie next time he's on, maybe say, doesn't he look a bit like Gloria with all those red curls, or just wait until I see an advert for his talk in the local library.'

'I'll have my fingers crossed until I get them back together.'

He left a very happy man.

I have run several sessions for couples who believe they have been together in previous lives and the story of Gunther and Helena that was shown to Paula and Drew Hammond was another one that brought tears to my eyes.
* * * * *

THE CUCKOO CLOCK

As Nadia stood at the bus stop, tapping her foot and glancing repeatedly at her wrist watch, she silently cursed the cuckoo clock for making her late and missing the bus to the local hospital.

It was an attractive, hand crafted, brightly painted, wooden cuckoo clock brought to England by Nadia's mother in 1938 when she and her Jewish parents had fled from the pre war chaos in Germany. Even though luggage was restricted Helena had insisted the clock was carefully packed into her suitcase.

Unfortunately it was, and always had been, totally unreliable

The clock had hung in the hall for decades and Nadia's mother was the only person who ever touched it. She dusted it carefully, wound it up and sometimes whispered to it.

Once, early in their marriage, Nadia's parents had missed the start of a film at the local cinema.

'We were late because of that crazy, incompetent cuckoo,' her father grumbled when he retold the story.

'His name is Gunther,' Helena quietly replied.

She never explained where the clock came from or why she called the bird Gunther.

The bus came. Nadia got on, flashed her pass, mumbled, 'City Hospital,' to the driver and took a seat.

She remembered when she and her brother, Henry, had attempted to catch Gunther

'We should try at midday,' said Henry, 'when he flies in and out twelve times.'

'Let's stand on these chairs and grab him as he comes out,' suggested Helena.

Their mother, heard the chairs being moved and rushed into the hall, where she found them with arms outstretched and fingers waiting to grab the cuckoo.

She pulled them away, quite roughly shouting, 'You could have broken him. NEVER, EVER touch my clock again.'

Nadia also recalled the day she found her distraught mother crying in the hall.

Tearfully Helena explained, 'At three o'clock Gunther flew out, cuckooed just once and then I heard a creaking noise. Now the doors won't close and the clock isn't ticking.'

Helena was depressed while the clock was being mended but the rest of the family were secretly glad of the silence.

When Helena went to collected her clock the horologist said, 'I 'm mystified. The clock is working again but despite being oiled and reconditioned, it's still not a reliable time keeper.'
Recently Nadia and her brother had been told that their mother was dying and they knew that soon the family house would need to be cleared and sold.

'Look at each item and decide bin, keep or donate,' a friend told her.

Gunther would definitely be one of the first things to go, but onto which pile? Nadia knew they would find it difficult to decide

When she reached the hospital she found her mother staring at the ceiling and sitting down beside her Nadia gently took her hand.

'Sorry I'm late,' she said, 'Gunther was running slow again and so I missed the bus.'

Helena's eyes opened wide and she smiled at Nadia. 'Ah Gunther.' she murmured. She looked at Nadia again, then let her gaze rest on a space near the door.

Ah, Gunther,' she sighed.

Then she smiled and closed her eyes for the last time.

In Southern Germany, Ludwig Schmitz's father drifted in and out of consciousness.

'He's had an amazing life ,' Ludwig said to a nurse, 'I've no idea how many clocks he's carved and painted and even though battery operated cuckoo clocks are now mass produced for the tourists there've always been people willing to pay for one of his traditionally made clocks.'

Suddenly his father whispered, 'I've been paid for every clock I ever made, except for one.'

'What happened to that one?' Ludwig asked.

His father's eyes filled with tears.

'It was a birthday present,' he said, 'for someone very special. But on the day I was regulating its mechanism she ran into my workshop and she was crying.'

'My parents say it isn't safe for us to stay here any longer,' she said, 'and so we are leaving for England tonight. My Darling, I've come to say goodbye.'

'I couldn't let her go without something to remember me by. So although it wasn't finished, I said, 'Happy Birthday for next Tuesday. I'll always love you and with my heart breaking in two, I gave it to her.'

Gunther opened his eyes and smiled at Ludwig.

'Ah, Helena, the girl with the touch of midnight in her eyes,' he murmured.

He looked at Ludwig again, then let his gaze rest on a space near the door.

'Ah Helena,' he sighed. He smiled and closed his eyes for the last time.

* * * * *

A touching love story.

We had no proof as to who was who in a previous life though we all hoped that Gunther and Helena had found themselves together again in this lifetime as Beth and Drew Hammond.

The mirror never failed to amaze me with the different techniques it used to tell people their stories.

Perhaps the most bizarre was when it showed what appeared to be a picture book, showing pictures of Philip Jefferies in several different occupations.

* * * * *

THE PICTURE BOOK

The book was leather bound and contained a series of pictures. Slowly it opened and the pages were turned by an invisible hand to reveal a series of pictures, each with a caption written beneath it.

The first picture depicted a man sitting by a stream and holding a metal pan. In the bottom of the container there was a mixture of pebbles and soil and glittering among them were tiny pieces of gold, shimmering in the sunlight.

The caption for the picture was, 'California 1850.'

The page turned to reveal a painting of a young coloured girl picking cotton. 'South Carolina 1766,' was written under it.

The third page showed a young woman with a straw basket strapped to her back. She appeared to be selecting and picking tea leaves. This happened, according to the title, in China in 1688

The next image was a pencil drawing showing a young man wearing a smock with his trousers tucked into boots and a spotted handkerchief around his neck. He had a pole over his right shoulder and there were two dead rabbits tied to it by their feet. Written beneath it were the words, 'Poacher Stephan, Russia 1917.'

As the page turned again we saw a distressing photograph labelled 'Auschwitz 1944.' It was a close up of a man in an SS uniform. His hand was pointing at a group of young women.

Quickly that page flipped over. On the left hand side there was an image of men and women wearing shifts and tunics. They had chains around their ankles.

The right hand page depicted a man wearing a toga. He appeared to be studying the slaves and written underneath the picture were the words, 'Julius Thaddeus choosing his new slaves. Rome 1st century AD.'

The last image was an illustration of a man wearing a loin cloth. The top half of his body covered with colourful designs. Round his head there was a wreath like band of feathers and he was holding a boomerang in his right hand. The caption read, 'New south Wales, Australia 1429.'

* * * * *

We sat in silence for maybe two minutes, somewhat overcome by what we had seen.

Finally I said, 'Well you seem to have lived in several different cultures and a common theme in several of those lives was that you were choosing something, a ripe tea leaf, a slave, cotton buds, a rabbit for supper. Can I ask what your job is in this life?'

Philip was still looking rather bemused by what he had seen.

'Actually I work for a large retail outlet, 'he said, 'and my main task is to attend fashion weeks around the world and choose,' he smiled, 'the items I think will be big sellers in our fashion departments.'

'So choosing is certainly in your DNA make up,' I said, ' and in those other lives we saw you were looking for other things, animals to poach, diamonds to make you rich and obviously something to throw your boomerang at.

'We both laughed but neither of us mentioned the picture we had seen labelled 'Auschwitz.'

THE GOTH
Alice the Goth was always wandering through the market at lunch time. We all called her that to distinguish her from the young woman who worked on the fruit and veg. Stall. We called her 'Our Alice'

Alice the Goth runs a local cafe called The Dark Cavern. It is a meeting place where those who dress as Goths can feel comfortable, knowing they won't be judged for their appearance, and a place where they can order such delicacies as a black latte or a blood cup cake, which I was relieved to hear, obtained its realistic colour from beetroot juice!

Alice the Goth stopped by my cubicle for a chat one lunch time.

'There's this gorgeous fellow started coming into the cafe every day,' she said.

'He always sits in the same seat, facing the window, orders a plain black coffee which he drinks really slowly and spends most of his time gazing out of the window. Sometimes he nods to those sitting nearby but he never engages in conversation with them.'

'He looks a bit out of place if I'm honest, with his blue jeans, black hoodie and black woollen hat. No make up, white trainers, (she shuddered at the thought) and not a tattoo in sight.'

'He hasn't quite mastered the Goth look. Anyway, several times he has turned towards the counter and caught my eye. '

'I smiled once and he winked back at me. So what I am wondering is could your mirror tell me if we went out together he'd be willing to change his look? I mean I couldn't be seen in public with someone in white trainers (she gave another shudder) but I really do fancy him.'

I felt sure this request was not something the mirror would be able to predict, but I suggested she sat down and said we would try and see if anything happened.

* * * * *

THE MAN IN THE HOODIE.
The man, who recently had come into the cafe every morning was not there today. The place was busy and a young woman dressed in a flowing black cloak was sitting in his usual chair, second one on the right after the door.

The man in question was strolling down the road trying not to look too conspicuous. He stopped outside the newsagents and studied the postcards displayed in the window, glanced at his watch and continued his walk down the parade of shops, until he met up with another hooded youth who was approaching who was outside Jackson's Jewellers.

As they both entered the shop, the driver of a car parked further up the street also glanced at his watch. He switched on the car's ignition, released the hand brake and pulling out of the parking space, drove slowly past the newsagents and pulled up outside the Jacksons.

At that precise moment a woman rushed into the cafe shouting loudly,

'I've just seen two men take guns out from under their hoodies and they pulled their woollen hats right over their faces before they went into Jackson's Jewellers.

Alice reached for her phone, dialled 112 and asked for the police.

There was panic in the cafe as some people rushed to the window to see what was going on and others lay down on the floor, scared they might get shot.

The man in the getaway car had kept his engine running but he didn't wait for his colleagues to emerge from the shop, once he heard the police car sirens. Luckily someone in the cafe managed to note down the registration number before the car sped away.

Alice the Goth was once of those who wanted to see what was happening. As she arrived at the doorway, three police cars, screeched to a halt outside the jewellers.

Policemen, all armed rushed out of the cars. Several went round the back of the property and the rest formed a semi circle in front of the shop door way.

Those watching in the cafe could hear one of the men shouting through a megaphone, informing the men inside that the building was surrounded by armed police and advising them to come out with their hands above their heads.

It was three hours later when the robbers finally emerged. Coffee and cakes from The Cavern had been sent in, at the request of the thieves and some were also given to the police, two ambulances crews and several reporters who were waiting outside.

Everyone in the cafe had been forbidden to leave and advised to move away from the windows.

Alice went back behind the counter and she just happened to be looking out the window as the man, with no Goth dress sense, came out of the jewellers with his hands in the air.

* * * * *

The mirror clouded over.

'I'm guessing the answer to my question is don't get involved with him,' said Alice. 'He is obviously sitting in the cafe casing the jewellers. What do I do now though, the police will never believe me if I tell them what we have just seen.'

'Actually one of them might,' I said. 'Ask for Jerry Lowler and tell him I gave you his name.'

Alice agreed and hurried back to The Cavern to ring the police.

As soon as she had gone I phoned Jerry, the policeman I had liaised with during 'the shopping trolley case,' to prepare him for her phone call.
Only Alice The Goth and I know that a plain clothes police man will be sitting in the third chair on the right from the door of The Dark Cavern for the next week or two, ready to alert the armed police when he sees the hooded man begins his stroll up the parade of shops!

Kit Weaver was a young man who had just graduated from catering college. He wanted to have a future life progression to see if there was any indication that he would ever have his own restaurant.

' As soon as I start work next week I plan to start putting some money aside each month to buy my own cafe or restaurant but I know I will work harder if I know I have something to work towards and I'll be truly motivated if I see myself in the future as a respected chef.'
* * * * *

THE RESTAURANT

One by one the master chef looked at each member of his staff in turn, and then lowered his eyes.

'I am ashamed of you all,' he said.

'Those of you who have just arrived may not know what I witnessed this afternoon, though I now suspect that all of you have known this happened from time to time and may even be guilty of doing it yourself.'

No one spoke and no one looked at anyone else. Several felt themselves blush.

Kit, the master chef lowered his voice, 'For over thirty-five years I have taken pride in every morsel of food that has been prepared and cooked in my kitchens.'

'I sent it out to the diners believing it to be a truly perfect dish about to enchant the taste buds of those eating here.'

'Of course over the years I have heard rumours from other establishments that chefs with vendettas may defile the food for a certain client they dislike or be asked to do so by one of the waiting staff.'

'Sadly I now have proof that I must have been naive, maybe during all of my career as a chef. Until today I have always trusted my staff and didn't believe, until I saw it with my own eyes, that it would ever happen in such a high class kitchen as mine, staffed by elite chefs.'

'I am afraid I will never be able to trust any of you again to cook and prepare for service an unpolluted plate of food. I cannot run the risk of my clients eating food that has been tampered with in such an unpleasant way.'

'I am sorry for the innocent amongst you. Those who came through the back way will not have seen the sign at the front.'

'The doors of Kit's Kitchen are now permanently closed and the ovens are all switched off. Future reservations will be cancelled because as of 3p.m. this afternoon I have retired from the catering business, forever!'

'You will all be given a very generous redundancy package and with the exception of one person, all of you will be given glowing references. I wish you luck in the kitchens where you find work in future.'
* * * * *

'Wow', said Kit as the picture faded from the mirror. 'Looks like I will have something more than just a snack bar and if my maths is right I should be running my own kitchen by my mid thirties, cos I reckon that was me we have just seen when I was, what would you say, in my sixties?'

I nodded in agreement and wished him good luck for his future as a chef. 'Maybe you are the next Jamie Oliver,' I said jokingly as he left.

Lesley also booked in for a future life progression. When she arrived she explained she had recently had a card reading from a local psychic.

She told me the cards showed a fall out with a very close relation of mine, but said if I was very careful it could be avoided. When I asked if she could be more specific about this fall out, she shook her head. So I am wondering if you can throw some light on it.

* * * * *

THE BORROWED BOOK

Lesley looked at the book she had just extracted from te back of the broom cupboard. The top corner of the front cover was bent and the whole book was very dusty. She flicker her duster over it and then gasped in dismay when she saw the title. This was the book that had caused the problem between her and with her twin sister.

The book, Cheryl swore she had lent her six or maybe seven months ago. The book, Lesley, had been adamant she had never set eyes, let alone read it. The book, she most definitely not borrowed and therefore still did not have. The book, that caused the fall out between them nearly three months ago when Cheryl had asked for it back.

Lesley opened the front cover and there, just as her sister had said, was an inscription in neat copper plate writing. ' To Cheryl, many thanks for all your hard work,' and under it was the scrawl of the author's signature.

She remembered her sister's excitement when she had got the researcher's job. How happy she had been reading through countless manuscripts and looking at ancient photos to find the information her employer needed for her latest novel. And how happy she had been when her hard work had enabled Christine Medway, the county's favourite crime write, to produce yet another number one best seller.

Now she also remembered Cheryl showing her the book and telling her she could read this special copy as long as she kept it safe and promised to never read it while she was eating soup.

Crime wasn't a genre that interested Lesley so she had never even started to read the book and had put it in this cupboard to keep it safe, forgotten about it and denied its existence.

* * * * *

As the scenario faded I turned to look at Lesley.

'That is truly uncanny,' she said. 'I do have a twin sister. At the moment she in unemployed and is searching for work. If what we have just seen is a true picture of what to come then it seems that at some point she will be lucky enough to get a job with an author.'

'The psychic did make a point of telling me that what she saw was one of several possible futures for me and that things can change depending on choices one makes. So what I must do is to make certain I never ever let Cheryl lend me a book and then we won't have cause to argue about it.'

'Thank you so much.'

THE LAST ONE.
The final client in June was a young woman called Wendy who had a dark red birth mark over three quarters of her face.

'I just want to know if anyone will every love me,' she said.

* * * * *

THE PERFORMER
The band was playing the intro music.

The audience collectively held their breath, they knew she was on her way.

A drum roll announced her arrival and Mouse Hennesy stepped onto the stage to tumultuous applause, whistles and cheers.

She wore five inch heels, fishnet stockings, a skimpy bejewelled outfit and of course her trade mark mouse mask. This too sparkled with diamonds, real ones of course and was a vibrant red, to match her costume.

She bowed to her audience and straight away launched into her first set of songs.

She was the darling of the music world, the welcome guest on any chat show and the idol America was waiting to welcome. Mouse, however, refused all offers to work outside of Britain.

Wendy Henessy lived in a small town just north of Sheffield. Although she had been there for six years her neighbours knew little about her.

They suspected she travelled with her job as she was often away from home for weeks at a time, but what that job was they didn't know.

They called her, 'The lady with the birth mark,' not in an unkind way but because they had no idea what her real name was.

No one guessed the somewhat frumpily dressed lady at number 6 was in fact the masked superstar Mouse Henessey.

Her brother drove her to all her performances and the transformation from Wendy with the birth mark to Mouse with her mask was always undertaken at a secret location.

Even the roadies who handled the equipment needed for her performances didn't know her true identity. When they met her at the venues she was always dressed as Mouse.

Performing in Britain was no problem but a visit the States would require that

she acquired a passport and that was something Mouse refused to do.
* * * * *

Wendy was smiling.

'It is my dream to sing in public,' she said.'

'I am sure what we have just seen would be impossible to implement successfully and doubt I'm good enough to hit the big time. Although one thing I'm certain of is the fact that I couldn't walk anywhere in five inch heels,' she laughed.

'I once went to a fancy dress party as a cat and I've still got the mask so what I have just seen has given me an idea as to how I might gain enough confidence to perform during open mike nights in local pubs and maybe if I start to go out more and the audience will love me and I might even meet my soul mate.'

She got up and gave me a hug.

'Watch this space,' she said as she waved goodbye.

Just two days ago I received the following letter;
Dear Lisa,
 I know you have many clients every month so, I don't know if you will remember me but I had a future life

regression with you last June and your mirror told the story of a singer called Mouse who, like me, had a disfiguring birth mark on her face.

It took me a couple of weeks to pluck up courage to attend my first open mike session but since then I have been singing in public every week.

I call myself Wendy Whiskers and always appear wearing my cat mask. I have built up quite a following and now instead of singing for free I am getting regular bookings at pubs and clubs.

I also want to let you know that through my singing I have met someone special and to tell you what happened last weekend.

My friend Brian suggested we went for an evening walk. There was an amazing sunset. The sky was dappled with many shades of pink and purple and the sun was reflected in the lake as an orange ball.

We sat on a wooden bench watching as the sun sank lower and lower seemingly slipping into the water of the lake.

Brian bent down and picked up a stone from those scattered around the bench. With a flick of his wrist he launched it towards the lake and as it bounced in and out of the coloured water he chanted, 'She loves me, she loves me not, she loves me.'

He leant back with relief and said, 'All those hours of practicing were worth while, I needed to try and make sure my skim ended with a, 'she loves me.'

The sun had almost completely disappeared as he rose from the bench and got down on one knee. He took a black velvet box from his pocket and squeezing my hand said, 'Wendy Whiskers will you marry me?'

As you can probably guess I said, 'Yes.'

So included with this letter is your invite to our wedding. Without you and your amazing mirror I would never have plucked up the courage to start my career as a singer, which led me to meeting Brian.

Thank You Wendy.xxx

So those were the experiences of some of my clients last June and by the end of the month most of my appointments for July had been booked.

It was certainly a lucky day for me when the TV company contacted the junk shop and then refused to buy that antique mirror.

What it has revealed over the last thirty days has answered questions, made people smile and given some clients hope for their possibly future.

I thought the above paragraph was the last one I was going to write, but the day after I had typed those words into the computer I had a message from a TV company.

They were asking if they could make a documentary about my work with the mirror and were offering a rather obscene amount of money for the privilege.

I made myself a cup of coffee and sat down to consider the offer and its implications.

Suddenly, I noticed that the mirror had misted over and as the fog slowly cleared I realised my rainbow curtains were not reflected in it. There was no image of the ribbons and flowers that covered the tarnished part of the mirror. My table and chairs were not there and nor was I. The unit was completely empty.

Was this a warning from the mirror about my future if I allowed that documentary to be made?

Other novels by Karen Roberts

The author is experiencing vivid dreams depicting the future of planet earth.

At the start of the 21st century an eminent professor predicts that a devastating crisis will extinguish all life on planet earth. Most of the human population ignore his words but a group, known as The Survival Federation implement plans to save, not only themselves, but a 'chosen few' as well. When civilization as we know it starts to break down some alien races take steps to save certain people. The story follows characters before, during and after The Crisis and depicts what life is like in the 25th century, just before disaster is set to strike the population once again.

Are these dreams just science fiction stories? Or is the author in contact with beings from the future, who hope that by telling these tales in dreamtime The Crisis can be avoided?

the spring of 2020

MARTHA, THE SEASIDE WRITER

During a family holiday by the sea
Martha discovers that the sound of the
waves sends her into a state of altered
consciousness during which she writes
amazing stories. She becomes famous
when an anthology of her work is
published. When the family return to
the coast, Martha's stories have
changed. They seemed interlinked and
channelled from actual people who tell
about the heart wrenching lives of
Karinda, a film star, her abusive
husband Matt and her lover Abe. Piecing
together information gleaned from these
stories Martha and her husband are able
to unite Abe with a daughter he never
knew existed.

Printed in Great Britain
by Amazon

66932404R00120